DEMONS AND TEA LEAVES

COURTNEY DAVIS

5 PRINCE PUBLISHING
5PRINCEBOOKS.COM

Cover design by Marianne Nowicki

Interior design by 5 Prince Publishing

First Edition 01142025

For more information about this title, visit:

www.5princebooks.com

To my family who is always there to support me as I write, plan to write, and talk about writing! All the stories in my head need out and sometimes you have to listen to them before I put them down on the computer.

Acknowledgments

Thank you to the 5 Prince team for giving me another chance to put my story out into the world, I am forever grateful for your confidence in my ability to deliver a story worth reading.

And thank you to my amazing editor Cate for taking my story and helping me to make it something to really be proud of.

Also by Courtney Davis

The Atlantis Series

The Vampires of Atlantis

Aristotle's Wolves

Descendants of Atlantis

Stand Alone Titles

Butterfly Kisses

The Serpent and the Firefly

A Spider in the Garden

Princess of Prias

Soul Sacrifice

A Shadow Among the Stars

Demons and Tea Leaves

DEMONS AND TEA LEAVES

CHAPTER
ONE

"Your grandmother was a wonderful woman."

Hailey smiled and nodded, saying thank you for what felt like the thousandth time to the thousandth familiar face. As the people moved past her, they reiterated the sentiment to her sister, Kathy, and then moved straight on to the food and tea. That's what they were all here for, the refreshments. Why did people have to eat at every event? Why couldn't they just come and grieve and leave? Why was there an expectation of food and drink? It certainly didn't make *her* feel any better about losing her grandmother, the woman who had raised her for so many years and supported her emotionally even into adulthood.

"Stop fidgeting," Kathy murmured and reached out with a gentle pinch to Hailey's arm.

Hailey dropped her hands from where they were tangled in front of her, pulling at the fabric of her boring black dress, and tried to focus on the next person coming up to say the exact same thing.

"Your grandmother was such a gifted tea sommelier; I came to her many times and she always had exactly what I needed."

"Yes she was," Hailey agreed. Although her grandmother

hadn't had an official shop, she'd sold teas out of her large Victorian home to anyone who showed up on her doorstep at any time of day or night. She claimed to be able to cure any ailment they came to her with. Too bad she'd never been able to cure Hailey of her anxiety. For that she'd only ever offered advice, *'Trust your gut, you have instincts untapped, listen to what it's trying to tell you. See what it's trying to show you.'*

"We have a nice selection of teas set out for you to enjoy," Kathy said. "My fiancée has kept it stocked for everyone with some of our favorites from our grandmother's collection."

"Wonderful!" the woman said with far too much enthusiasm for a wake. Her name was Charlotte Bennington, and she had been a schoolteacher until she retired a few years ago. Hailey remembered her coming around and buying teas throughout the years, but Charlotte certainly never showed up to hang out with Hailey's grandmother. None of these people had, which made this whole scenario even harder for Hailey to understand.

"Where's the food going?" A young woman asked, stepping forward with a covered dish and a contrite smile. "I know I'm a little late to contribute, but better late than never, right?"

The one saving grace to all these people being here was that many of them had provided the food that was laid out for everyone to indulge in.

"Over there," Kathy pointed and the woman was off without even an attempt at condolences.

"Why the hell did she even bother to show up?" Hailey grumbled.

"Calm down, Hailey, these people are here showing their respect for Grandma, not us."

Hailey glanced around at the happy chattering people eating and talking. "I'm not sure about that." It wasn't supposed to be a happy occasion, this was a wake, but there was an air of celebration among many of the mourners that annoyed Hailey. She watched as a couple of older women dressed all in black with plates of food smiled and whispered by the bookcase. They even had the audacity to reach up and touch one or two as if closely reading the spines. Hailey wished she could tell them all to leave, to get out and let her begin the process of grieving that she needed to go through, that she couldn't even start until all this ceremonial crap was over.

"Girls, how are you holding up?" Mr. Rampart hobbled forward with a cane and a look of deep sadness on his wrinkled face.

"Mr. Rampart, I'm so glad you could make it," Hailey said, and she actually meant it this time. She gave him a hug.

"I am so sorry you two don't have your parents here to help with this. It shouldn't fall to the grandchildren."

"No, it shouldn't," Kathy agreed, giving the old man who had taught them both history in high school a hug as well.

"I remember coming here for your parents' wake. I think that was the last time I was in this house."

Hailey felt tears prickle her eyes at the reminder of this familiar scenario, a wake in her grandmother's house. The last one had been for their parents who'd passed away in a car accident when she was ten. It was what had led to Hailey and Kathy living with their grandmother for the rest of their childhood and why they'd become so close to the matriarch.

"Please enjoy a bite to eat and some tea, can I help you?" Kathy asked.

"Oh yes, my granddaughter is just parking the car," Mr. Rampart agreed with a wide smile and Kathy walked away with him, leaving Hailey to greet the next person.

She wasn't excited to see the face coming in the door. Cynthia Weatherbee had been in Hailey's graduating class and mentally never left high school. Cheerleader and skank. She'd always been after Hailey's boyfriends, not that Hailey had many to speak of.

"Hailey, alone as usual I see," Cynthia sneered and looked around dramatically to emphasize that fact. "I did hear you were single again, or is it, still?"

Hailey gritted her teeth, she hadn't had a serious boyfriend in a long time. That fact didn't bother her usually, she knew better than to settle for less than she deserved. Not only that, but so often when she'd mentioned the name of a guy she thought about dating to her grandmother the woman would give a negative opinion. Hailey had learned early on to trust her grandmother's beliefs about people's true selves no matter that the woman never offered an explanation along with it.

"I don't need a man to make my life worthwhile, Cynthia, I have..." what did she have? Not a good job and now Kathy was her only family. "I have all this," Hailey said waving her hand vaguely.

"Oh yeah, you keeping the old woman's stuff? Going to start selling teas in your spare time? That should make the men start running," Cynthia laughed and walked away.

"How did such a nice man have such a witchy granddaughter?" Kathy asked, returning to Hailey's side.

"I don't know but I can't believe of all the bitchy girls in our school, grandma had always had nice things to say about that one."

"You think she's good somewhere deep down?" Kathy asked.

Their gazes met and they both shook their heads.

Mrs. Hilltop approached after a few minutes with a scowl on her face. "Cynthia Weatherbee said you're planning to take over where your grandma left off, living here, making tea," she accused, pointing a gnarled finger in Hailey's face.

Hailey was struck dumb in the face of the accusation.

Kathy was quick to respond, thankfully. "We don't know what Grandma intended. We haven't even heard from the lawyer yet about what she put in the will, but no, I don't think either of us has Grandma's gift for teas or gardening, unfortunately."

Mrs. Hilltop narrowed her eyes at Hailey. "Fine, I'll be interested in coming by before the estate sale," she said and wandered off, back to a group of older women who seemed to be waiting for a report back.

"What the fuck is wrong with people?" Hailey hissed under her breath. She felt her anxiety start to ramp up and her hands went back to the front of her dress. She wanted to get away from all these people, this whole situation just didn't feel right. It didn't feel like her Grandma, Merry Honeycomb-Silver. Their grandma hadn't entertained most of these people on a regular basis, had in fact scowled and rolled her eyes at most of them when they passed on the streets of Lavender Grove or after they left her grandmother's house with their specialty tea purchase in hand.

But in her last days, Grandma had insisted that Hailey and Kathy do this, that they; *Let the community say goodbye and cut ties with her earthly presence.*

Hailey didn't give a shit about all this ceremony and tradition, and she knew Kathy didn't either. They weren't religious, they weren't ones for most traditions even, but they both knew their grandmother had been. She'd been strictly traditional, though her traditions had been unconventional; she was sure to always leave a window cracked at night to let the day's bad energy escape, and to sprinkle salt across the threshold when it stormed, and if a black cat approached you, *always* greet it kindly, because you never knew what was under their fur. And when someone died in the family, you held a wake and let whoever wanted to say goodbye, come and say goodbye otherwise their souls could remain unsettled, tied to their earthly possessions.

So that's what they were doing. It didn't mean Hailey had to like it.

"How are you two holding up?" Summer Long, Kathy's longtime partner and soon to be wife came up as there was a lull in the reception line.

"I think I might puke," Hailey admitted. "Why are there so many people here, not even half of them were at the funeral service or the burial."

"It's a small town and your grandmother lived here all her life, so everyone knew her. Besides, she was a popular woman, weren't these all people who bought her teas?" Summer asked in a soothing voice.

"Seems like it," Kathy said. "I remember a lot of these faces from our time living here. Of course, a lot of these people have also come into the shop and bought jewelry from us, too." Kathy designed jewelry for Summer's family's jewelry shop in downtown Lavender Grove. She was quite successful and mostly self-taught, designing things intricate and beautiful just like she'd always wanted.

Now that she'd mentioned it, Hailey recognized a few of Kathy's pieces on the women here today.

Kathy had made a name for herself in this town, creating things. It wasn't tea, but it was something and the reminder that Hailey didn't even come close to either her sister or her grandmother in this type of innate career ability just made her more annoyed.

"It's nice that they are here paying their respects," Summer said soothingly. She was always diplomatic and often inserted herself between the sisters. "Do either of you want me to get you something to eat?" Summer offered.

Hailey shook her head. "I can't stand the thought of food. Or these people, why the hell are they still here?"

"Why don't you take a break," Kathy suggested. "I can handle any more offers of condolence."

"No, I'm doing okay. This is important," Hailey said, remembering feeling a similar desire to escape when it had been her parents' wake. She hadn't run away from it then though either. She'd stood next to her sister and grandmother and accepted the condolences of probably mostly all these same people.

She hadn't thought that this many people were close enough to show up for Merry though, Hailey wasn't sure her grandmother *had* any really close friends at all.

And that was kind of a sad thing to realize. Merry had seemed content though in her mostly solitary life and Hailey visited often, so did Kathy. They were all still living in Lavender Grove after all, so they'd seen each other at least once a week.

But not anymore. Now she'd never get to spend time with her grandmother again and it hurt, a lot.

"You are starting to tremble, you need to go relax, I'll be fine here, I'll take care of everything," Kathy said.

Normally Hailey didn't resent her sister for her ability to handle any situation with grace, in fact she loved everything about Kathy and wanted the best for her. Hailey just wished sometimes that Kathy wouldn't look at her with those sad eyes as if she were wishing Hailey would grow up and get her own shit together finally, so Kathy didn't have to worry about her. Her grandmother had never worried about her, Hailey was sure that was why they'd gotten along so well. Kathy still insisted on mothering Hailey, despite her being twenty-nine years old.

"I'm okay, you shouldn't have to take care of all this on your own," Hailey said.

"I'm not alone, I have Summer."

The unsaid *and you have no one*, made Hailey fist her hands.

"You know what, I think I will take a little break from all this," Hailey said wanting to get away from her sister as much as everyone else in the room. She didn't make it far before she was stopped by a grey-haired woman with a frown on her face. Mrs. Jenson was a neighbor and had been one of the first to show up for the wake, Hailey was surprised she was still there.

"When is the estate sale?"

"Excuse me?" Hailey was taken aback by the harsh question.

"The estate sale. You two aren't planning to keep this place are you? It's too much for you young women. The gardens need constant attention, and the house is so large, cleaning it must be a nightmare. With jobs, you two would never be able to keep up, best to sell it all."

Mrs. Jenson wasn't wrong, the house was big. There was a stretch of yard out front and a beautiful garden her grandmother had taken great care to cultivate usefully. Flower and herb beds were everywhere with walkways between and out to the white picket fence that surrounded the property. It had always been a haven for Hailey and she wasn't looking forward to letting it go but she also wasn't sure she could handle it.

"We haven't decided yet."

"Well, let me know. Your grandmother had a lot of nice things."

Hailey wanted to growl at the woman—the vulture, that's what she was—and as Hailey looked back at the large living room full of people with that thought in mind, it was far too easy to see a scheming glint in the eyes of many guests.

"You're a good girl, you'll let me know. I could come through and maybe help decide what is worth selling if you want. Mrs. Hilltop might think she knows what things are worth, but she doesn't. Give me a call. My son in law works for an antiques shop."

Hailey didn't want to sell any of it, but she doubted she'd have a choice. "Sure thing, Mrs. Jenson."

Mrs. Jenson smiled brightly and walked away with as much of a spring in her step as someone of her age was capable of. Hailey didn't miss the glare Mrs. Hilltop sent her way. What was up with those two? Clamoring to get first pick through Hailey and Kathy's grief.

Hailey hurried to get out of the room before she had to talk to anyone else. She made her way up the stairs past dozens of family photos. Pictures that followed Hailey's father from birth all the way through to a final family photo of the four of them taken just a few months before her parents' passing. Hailey took after her father and grandmother in her looks with black hair and brown eyes that were nothing remarkable, not like Kathy with her blonde locks and green eyes, so much like their mother's. Hailey couldn't help reaching out to touch the gold frame near her mother's face before continuing upstairs. It was all photos of Hailey and Kathy after that.

She entered a room she'd stayed in many times as a child when she and Kathy had spent the night so their parents could have a date without kids and then all of her preteen and teen years after her parents died. It smelled the same, like lavender and dust, so familiar and comforting. She'd spent so many years in the room it felt like her own in a way that the memories of her childhood room in her parents' small house no longer did. This room still had the same bed she'd slept in for all those years, the same dresser with its top drawer that squeaked, and inside it a scratched-out name that she didn't know who belonged to; *Vint.* She'd asked her grandmother about it once, but the woman had just shrugged and changed the subject. Hailey had assumed the dresser must have been bought second hand and Vint was someone who'd owned it before. She'd run her finger over the lines of that name many times, wondering about the person with such an interesting name. The name of a man on the inside of her underwear drawer had felt so naughty and fun as a teen.

"Shit, now I'll never know the secret of that name," she whispered into the empty room. She let out a sigh, knowing she was going to have to clear out any personal things in this room, not something she was looking forward to. And Mrs. Hilltop and Mrs. Jenson's reminders that the time was limited pushed Hailey to open those drawers and look for lost treasures from her childhood.

She pulled out a few pairs of socks and revealed a sticker for a band she'd liked that she'd stuck under her underwear so her grandmother wouldn't see it. Her grandmother had thought the lead singer of *Devil's Dirty Gun,* a local punk band, was the worst kind of human, said he projected a false façade, and hated Hailey having anything to do with the music. Which of course had made Hailey like them all the more and even sneak out to a few shows. But then the band dissolved because the lead singer got arrested for armed robbery where he killed one man and wounded another. It was one of the first times Hailey had realized that her grandmother's gut feelings about people were usually right.

The sticker had stayed though, maybe a tribute to her ability to make her own mistakes, or maybe a reminder that her grandmother knew things Hailey didn't.

She laughed aloud at her childish bravery as she tossed the socks in a nearby garbage and shut the drawer. The rest of the dresser was equally half full of unnecessary items. Just random things she'd left behind and didn't care about enough to search for but her grandmother had washed, folded, and put away just in case she needed something when she was there next. Her grandmother was always doing little things to make other people's lives easier like that. She'd always been thinking of others, no matter the time of day.

Hailey had many happy memories of waking up from bad dreams and walking downstairs to find her grandmother up and making tea. She'd hand Hailey a cup as if she'd known Hailey would show up needing it and listen to her talk all about the dream. And with each word and sip of the sweet hot liquid, Hailey had felt the fear just disappear. Then her grandmother would send her back to bed with a fresh sprig of lavender to put on her windowsill to keep out *'bad vibes thrown around by people who should mind their own business.'* And Hailey would sleep well the rest of the night, waking rested.

Sometimes she'd wake up because of the voices of customers downstairs. Maybe it was an old lady thing to be up at night fiddling around in the kitchen with herbs.

Never again, Hailey reminded herself.

Tears stung Hailey's eyes and she closed them, taking a deep breath. Hailey walked to the window and picked up the old sprigs of lavender set there, inhaling their familiar scent. They were fairly fresh in contrast to the layer of dust on the sill. Her grandmother had never been an exceptional housekeeper, something about not wanting to throw out all the good luck with the dust, or so she'd said as an excuse.

This window looked out over the front yard, and Hailey saw a few more cars pull up, smiling faces that turned to somber ones as the people approached the front steps. It wouldn't be proper to not have a good funeral face on before entering the house and offering condolences to the bereaved. It was all fake though, Hailey could clearly see that. They would all go about their lives as if nothing had changed as soon as this socially dictated ordeal was over.

Her cellphone rang and she dug through her purse for the

thing she should have just turned off for the day. She grimaced when she saw the name on the screen. Her boss was calling. The asshole knew today was the wake. She'd been clear that she'd not be in any sooner than tomorrow. He was probably going to ask her to cover an evening shift or something.

She couldn't even imagine going back into the hotel and standing behind a desk listening to entitled guests complain about scratchy sheets or not enough shampoo.

She hit ignore and then turned the ringer off and stuffed it back in her purse.

That was just another thing she was putting off dealing with. Kathy was right, she needed to get her shit together. She dropped onto the familiar bed and buried her face in the pillow. It wasn't that she wanted to lose her job but it felt like she was standing at the edge of a cliff, and she wasn't sure if she was supposed to jump or turn and walk away. So she couldn't move at all, frozen with indecision because she didn't even know what the choices were that she was supposed to be choosing from.

Kathy insisted it was stress induced anxiety, possibly depression, and told her to go see the doctor about some kind of pill that might help. Hailey knew it wasn't something a pill could fix, an opinion her grandmother had encouraged. Hailey just didn't know what could fix it, other than having her grandmother reappear and make a cup of tea.

CHAPTER
TWO

When Hailey opened her eyes again it was dusk and the sounds of voices from downstairs were gone. She sat up and ran a hand through her hair wondering how she'd managed to sleep at all, let alone for what must have been three or four hours. Why hadn't Kathy woken her up? People were going to think she was rude for not being present.

She stopped that thought in its tracks. She didn't care what they thought of her, they didn't really know her, they weren't her friends.

When she made her way down the stairs, she heard Kathy and Summer talking quietly in the kitchen. She followed their voices and found the two sitting close at the table with an open bottle of wine.

"Hey! You're up," Kathy said, standing quickly and embracing her.

"Yeah, I can't believe I slept so long."

"I can. You haven't slept much since Grandma got sick," Kathy pointed out and frowned, as if berating a child for eating too much chocolate.

It was true though. Their grandmother had gotten sick

about a week ago—well, it was about a week ago that she had finally told her granddaughters that she was sick—and it had progressed fast from there. Hailey had come to stay for a day or two just to keep her company and make soup, but it had become obvious immediately that their grandmother wasn't going to just get better this time. Once Hailey had seen that, she'd been afraid to sleep, or even leave her grandmother's side for more than a few minutes. And so Hailey had been burnt out before she'd even had to start with the process of planning the funeral, something Kathy had pointed out immediately.

Thankfully Summer had taken on most of the arrangements since she wasn't as bereaved, but Hailey knew that Kathy had been by Summer's side all along, helping confirm decisions. Neither of them had asked for Hailey's input, which is how her grandmother had ended up buried in a hideous grey dress that Hailey knew her grandmother had hated. Hailey would have put her in something bright to match her personality, maybe red or purple, the woman had always preferred bright, rich colors. 'Life is too short to dress for anyone but yourself' she'd always said. Hailey had agreed wholeheartedly and found herself gravitating toward bright colors for herself as well, even in a professional setting she would throw a bright yellow blouse under a suit jacket and put on a pair of gold pumps, just to cheer herself up while she stood behind the front desk at work greeting people.

"I guess it was time to catch up a little," Hailey said.

"Yeah, it was," Kathy said.

Hailey stared into her sister's green eyes. She was so beautiful, even in funeral wear. Her long blonde hair curled and flowing to her mid back, her skin smooth and pale, her lips a subdued beige. She was so put together; it kind of irritated Hailey, she never looked that effortlessly beautiful.

Summer poured a glass of wine for Hailey, and she accepted it thankfully.

"You two sit and drink. I'll dish up some leftovers from the wake. I am certain you both need to eat," Summer said, comfortably taking control. Summer was just as tall as Kathy but with short black hair and deep brown eyes that showed her every emotion. She was so caring and wonderful; her sister had really lucked out there. Hailey had never been able to find someone that made her feel even half of what she saw between those two. It was the kind of love that she'd remembered seeing between their parents and what she wanted for herself someday. It was probably why she'd never been able to keep a relationship going; as soon as she saw it wasn't everything, she dropped it, not wanting to waste anyone's time.

Hailey sat in silence with Kathy, and they ate what Summer put in front of them without really caring what it was. She'd eaten a bite of toast that morning but that was all, and her stomach was thankful for the nutrition.

"The lawyer is meeting us here tomorrow. He'll read the will and have the paperwork we'll need to sign," Kathy said when Summer picked up their empty plates.

Hailey took a breath and nodded. Kathy had it all organized, all figured out and Hailey just had to go along. She knew Kathy thought she was doing Hailey a favor, making it easy. No stress for her anxiety-prone sister. "Okay." Hailey looked around and made a snap decision. "I'm not going back to work for another week so we should be able to get things mostly settled before then."

Kathy and Summer shared a look that Hailey didn't have the energy to decipher but she imagined it was along the lines of, *poor Hailey, can't handle any of this.*

"Are you about ready to head home?" Kathy asked Hailey,

reaching across the table and laying a hand on hers. "I think we are."

"No, I think I'm going to stay here tonight actually," Hailey said, making another sudden decision. She didn't want to leave this place just yet. As soon as she said it, a knot released in her belly. It was the right decision.

"Alone?" Kathy asked, surprised.

Hailey had gone back to her apartment after her grandmother passed but tonight, it felt right to stay.

"I'm alone in my apartment too, Kathy, I don't need a babysitter."

"I know I just—" Just then the large grandfather clock in the front room chimed seven. Kathy clamped her lips and nodded. "Okay, Hay, we'll leave you here if you're sure."

Kathy didn't usually use the old nickname and it eased Hailey's annoyance a little. She knew her sister wanted the best for her.

"This is pretty well cleaned up. There's definitely food for you to eat in the morning but we'll bring lunch when we come to meet with the lawyer," Summer said as she started the dishwasher.

"I am perfectly capable of taking care of myself, been doing it for years," Hailey grumbled.

"You are still my baby sister," Kathy said, standing and embracing Hailey from behind her chair. "We will bring lunch, and we will see you about noon. The lawyer is supposed to be here at one. Call if you need anything."

"You aren't working tomorrow either?" Hailey asked, surprised. Summer practically ran the store for her parents at this point and Kathy loved what she did so much she rarely took a day off herself.

"We are both going in for a few hours in the morning, but we'll be off by lunch."

"I'm glad, you'll feel better being back to routine and your creative outlet," Hailey said, smiling at her sister. Kathy was so talented, the pieces she created were amazing and everyone fell in love with them instantly. She did some custom orders, but what really shone, were the things she came up with all on her own. There was nothing like them.

Hailey wished she had a creative career, but that would mean she'd have finally settled into something at all. She'd bounced around from low-paying job to medium-paying job her entire adult life. Now at twenty-nine, she felt like the pressure was on to find something she could make a life doing.

What she didn't want to tell Kathy and Summer, was that her manager was hinting around about replacing her if she didn't show up in the next few days. It seemed that the caretaking of her grandmother in her last days had used up all Hailey's leave time, and now, she just needed to suck it up and get back to the grind.

But she couldn't. She felt hollow and she knew that the cure wasn't working behind a desk and telling other people that she was—*so sorry about that*—when they complained that they didn't have the perfect experience with their check-in.

She needed something else, maybe it was time to finally figure out what she was going to do with her life. She wished her grandmother was here to talk to about it. Merry would have made her some tea and they'd have sat on the sunporch, even at night, and talked through options and wants and desires and most importantly, gut feelings. What did Hailey feel right about?

Summer set down the rag she'd used to wipe up the crumbs in the kitchen and looked expectantly at Kathy.

Kathy gave Hailey one last squeeze then straightened. "Alright, see you tomorrow."

. . .

Once alone, Hailey waited for regret to set in, waited to feel like she should have taken them up on the offer of a ride home and been in her own comfortable apartment tonight. But it didn't come, she felt right being here.

"Hope you don't mind, Grandma, but I like it here," she said to the empty house.

They hadn't officially decided what to do with the place, but she knew what Kathy wanted. After the lawyer read out the details of the will tomorrow, they'd probably have some major decisions to make. Kathy wanted to sell the place and most of its antiques, split the money, maybe take a vacation or use her half for her and Summer's wedding and honeymoon. Hailey would be able to have savings, maybe put a down payment on a little place of her own.

But Hailey couldn't imagine losing this place like that. She also couldn't afford to buy her sister out of it, or even pay the yearly taxes, she imagined. Not with the kind of jobs she usually had which paid just enough to keep the credit cards settled and food on her table.

Maybe selling would give her the freedom to look for a job that really felt right instead of taking whatever was offered first. That would be a new experience for her.

Feeling hopeless, Hailey started some water boiling in the familiar kettle then rummaged through the tea cabinet for the one she wanted.

It was what her grandmother always made her when she was feeling worried about the future. Hailey wasn't sure what exactly was in it, but it had a sweet and spicy flavor and it always managed to settle her nerves. She found it in a glass container marked as *Stress Relief* in her grandmother's handwriting. Hailey ran a finger across the scrawled letters and almost felt her grandmother's presence behind her.

"I guess I should be careful how much of this I use, you

won't be making more this year, will you?" Hailey whispered into the empty room. There was a lot in the jar as well as jars and jars of other teas and herbs in multiple cabinets of the kitchen, and a whole room in the house where dried and drying herbs were kept. Her grandmother's life, for as long as Hailey had known her, had been spent working with herbs, teas, and edible flowers. The house was full of the evidence. It was more than Hailey could imagine trying to take back to her apartment. But the thought of throwing any of it out twisted Hailey's gut, her grandmother had always said that waste was a sin. Who would want it all besides her, though? Maybe she could sell some of it at an estate sale. Which was a whole other issue because she didn't like the idea of her grandmother's things, her furniture, dishes, rugs and decorations going anywhere. It just felt wrong to let go of the items her grandmother had collected over a lifetime. These were the last pieces of the woman who had raised her during the hardest parts of her childhood.

"What the hell am I supposed to do?" Hailey said as she made her cup of tea, hoping her problems and worries would be solved in its warmth as she'd experienced so many times in this house.

By the time she settled into the couch with the steaming cup and the television remote in hand, the glow of twilight had dimmed to barely anything as it filtered through the front windows.

One sip of the flavorful tea and Hailey felt the familiar relaxation settle over her.

She turned on the television and let her mind blank as she stared at the show she'd seen multiple times.

"I knew exactly what to do. But in a much more real sense, I had no idea what to do."

Hailey let out a sigh at the familiar and comforting

dialogue. Maybe it was a result of her anxiety, but watching the same show over and over never got old for her.

The clock sounded, letting her know it was eight. Her tea was almost gone and cold, the sun had completely disappeared, and just when she thought she might shower and head to bed early, there was a knock at the front door.

Hailey stood so fast her tea spilled on the carpet.

"Fuck," she hissed, frozen with indecision for a moment. Did she answer the door or clean up the spill?

The knock sounded again and pulled her into action. She hurried to the door, ready to send away the condolence giver with a frown, why the hell would they show up this late?

The front door was solid and there were no windows around it to let her know who might be waiting on the front porch, she'd always thought it a mistake in the design and had even tried to convince her grandmother once or twice to have a different door put in or at least a small window for safety reasons.

Her grandmother had insisted that there wasn't a safer place in the world than inside her house and so there was nothing to fear on the other side of the front door.

"Just don't invite evil inside," her grandmother had added with a laugh.

Hailey took a deep breath and opened the door.

She was struck dumb by the sight that met her there. It was a man she'd never seen before—she definitely would have remembered him—which meant he was likely a lost stranger to the town asking for directions. He was tall, broad across the shoulders, and frankly, angry looking. His strong jaw seemed tight, lips pursed in irritation and his dark eyes scowled down at her. He had a hood over his hair, but she could see locks of long brown poking out around his shoulders. If she were to guess, she'd say he was in his mid-to-late thirties and definitely her type.

Well, maybe her type if he didn't look like he wanted to murder her. Hailey moved hastily to shut the door before even asking him what the hell he wanted.

"Don't shut the door, I need to get in there," the man said with a gruff voice.

"To murder me? No thanks," she snapped and slammed the door.

"Good choice, he had a look about him that was pure sex mixed with anger, not always a good combination."

Hailey spun around at the unfamiliar and entirely unexpected voice, then screamed when she came face to face with a translucent woman in a black and white maid's uniform. She looked to be in her fifties and had a stern set to her mouth.

The ghost disappeared with a screech just as the door behind Hailey burst open and the man in question stepped inside with a knife in his grip. Hailey took one look at the murderer now inside the house and ran.

She didn't make it far. She was just inside the living room where she was hoping to reach her cell phone when his arm wrapped around her middle and her back was pressed against his front.

"Just listen," he snarled.

"To a psycho? Do you think I'm crazy?"

"I think you're in danger, but not from me," he insisted.

Just then another ghost, this one a man, appeared in the room with them. He was wearing a black waistcoat, long in the back, with a white button up underneath and black slacks. His grey hair was slicked back, and he held himself stiff, hands clasped behind him.

"You are frightening the maid, and she won't work if she is frightened," he chastised Hailey.

Hailey opened her mouth and closed it, unsure what the hell was going on but wondering if that tea had been laced with something to give her these hallucinations.

"Sorry Drandy," the potential murderer said, not releasing his hold on her.

The ghost dressed as a butler huffed and disappeared.

Next thing Hailey knew, another ghost maid, this one younger, was cleaning up the tea Hailey had spilled.

"I'm dreaming," Hailey whispered.

"No," the man said. "If I let you go, are you going to run and scream again? Or are you going to listen?"

"Are you going to still be trying to murder me?" she countered.

"I was never trying to murder you. I heard you scream and came in to help you."

Hailey wanted to argue but she couldn't deny it could have been as he said. "Why are you here so late, the wake was over hours ago."

He let her go and she jumped away, spinning around to face him while quickly putting the couch between them. His hood had fallen down while he was holding her, and she bit her lip as she took in the full sight of him. His dark hair was shaggy, reaching just above his shoulders, and on top of his head two small black horns shone in the light.

Her foot landed in a spot still damp from her spilled tea and she remembered it wasn't very wet because a fucking ghost had taken care of it and now, she was looking at someone who had horns.

It was too much, and she felt her heart speed, her throat tighten, and her vision go black. "I should have taken those pills Kathy suggested," she managed to mutter as she realized that she'd finally broken herself. Anxiety-induced delusions were a definite reason to try some prescription drugs.

"Shit," she heard the possible murderer snap as she began to fall, but she didn't hit the floor. Something caught her just before she would have likely smacked her head on the coffee table.

CHAPTER
THREE

Vint frowned down at the woman passed out in his arms. This was not how he'd planned on tonight going. In fact, he hadn't planned on interacting with her at all. Why was she still here? Merry was dead, the wake was over, and surely Hailey and her sister were planning to cut loose and sell everything as soon as possible. It was why he'd been sure to get here tonight, before anyone else could.

"Are you planning to hold her until she wakes up?" Drandy asked stiffly, reappearing in the room.

He was tempted to say yes. She felt good in his arms, soft and warm. Her face, now that it wasn't twisted in fear or accusations of murder, was intriguing. Full, red lips and smooth, sun-kissed skin. Her nose was small and pert and there was a freckle there on the side of her nose that begged to be kissed. A man would want to spend time on this face, learning its nuances, feathering kisses along her dark lashes and nuzzling her rounded cheeks.

Drandy cleared his throat and Vint stiffened, those were very dangerous thoughts.

Vint snapped his eyes to the ghost and frowned. "You know

it would have helped if you and the maids had acted like you all had a clue as to who I was, old man," Vint snarled at the ghost.

Vint thought he saw a slight lift to the old ghost's lips. "Merry never wanted her granddaughters to know about you, why would I go against her wishes even if she *is* on my side of the living now?"

Vint barely controlled the urge to roll his eyes. "You know that wasn't Merry's idea. She was bound by an oath. An oath that's dead as her now, which is why Hailey was able to see you three I might add. So keeping me from her is no longer an issue." And why did that statement feel so raw and real?

Drandy made a sound that Vint wasn't sure was agreement or not.

Vint turned and started up the stairs, annoyed with himself. Merry had kept this meeting from happening while she was alive and he'd often wondered if it was more than the promise to her son, had she believed he would be a bad influence on her precious granddaughters? He didn't even blame her for it. His kind was dangerous, and this woman was ... tempting, delectable, beautiful.

He felt the heat of her body against his chest, his arms holding her a little closer even as he told himself he should just set her on the couch and walk away. But her head was resting against his shoulder, and her breath fanned his neck making him want to keep her there forever.

Vint growled, forcing his thoughts away from that path and stared ahead as he trudged up the stairs. He had no idea how long Hailey would be out, but she might as well be comfortable while she slept. He doubted she'd like waking up in his arms, judging by the way she'd freaked out at seeing his horns.

At least this was the definitive sign that she was indeed Merry's blood, and the oath was no longer keeping her vision clouded to that of a regular human. He remembered Hailey's dark eyes narrowing on him suspiciously when he stood on the porch, she had been afraid, not trusting him on instinct. Most non-magical humans naturally distrusted him too, but they didn't react so strongly, because they couldn't pinpoint the 'otherness' he exuded. She'd seen it though, and she hadn't liked it even if she hadn't known why.

The way she'd reacted fiercely in the living room had shown her fire, he hadn't expected that, and it intrigued him more than he would have expected. Her passing out on sight of his horns, now that had been what he had expected and been trying to avoid by knocking politely with his hood up when he noticed the lights on in the house.

Vint shifted her slightly in his arms as he topped the stairs, his hands settling into the softer curves of her body. She wasn't heavy, but she was warm and soft, and he liked the way she felt pressed against him. He shouldn't like the feel of her against him but the thought lingered, all the same.

Annoyed now and with his hands full, he kicked open the door to the room he knew was hers. This was the younger sister, Hailey, and she'd stayed in the room that had once been so familiar to him. He laid her on the bed and stepped back, letting his eyes slide up the length of her pantyhose-clad legs sticking out from the very plain black dress she wore. It didn't hide curves he'd just spent time admiring the feel of and he fisted his hands to keep from tracing each one with a finger.

"Sir, it isn't proper for you to stare at a sleeping lady," Valerie, the elder maid that haunted the place, chastised from behind him.

"I'm not staring, I'm trying to decide if she's going to try and kill me when she wakes up."

"You know, she might. She is a tough young woman, always has been," Valerie teased. "Much more emotionally driven than her sister."

Vint rolled his eyes and left the room. "Let me know when she wakes up. I think we need to have a talk."

"Yes sir," Valerie said, "I'll have Sarah keep a watch. Are you planning to stay the night? Should we prepare the other room?"

"No, I won't be sleeping tonight I have a feeling." There was too much to watch out for. It was why he was here. The spells, the guards, the hexes and the wards; everything Merry had ever done that connected directly with herself were all officially burnt out. Today's wake had cut the last tie, and unfortunately, he wasn't the only one who knew it.

"Why is she staying here?" he asked Valerie as he strode down the hallway.

Valerie and the other two ghosts had been with Merry ever since he'd known her, which was basically since he was born. He trusted them and knew that they had been utterly devoted to Merry and knew everything that went on in this house.

He wondered briefly what would become of them if a regular family moved in, people who would never see or interact with the ghosts who resided here, but maybe would sense them every now and again and get a shiver unexpectedly in a warm room. Would the ghostly inhabitants slowly fade away?

"She's sad, I think she's taking Merry's passing harder than Kathy. Of course, Kathy has someone to hold onto, poor Hailey is all alone, and she feels things so deeply. It's always been her blessing and curse."

Vint nodded and walked downstairs. He wanted to check the doors and windows, make sure everything was locked up tight.

Hailey rolled over and snuggled down into her pillow, inhaling the scent that meant she was in her grandmother's house. She shifted and frowned into the pillow realizing she was still wearing her wake outfit, pantyhose and all. She hated pantyhose, what the hell was she doing sleeping in them? Why hadn't she showered before bed like usual?

What ... then it all came back, the knock, the ghosts, the fucking horns!

She gasped and sat up in bed. The room was dark except for the moonlight coming in through the window, enough light to show that she wasn't alone.

Two ghostly maids were staring down at her curiously.

"She's awake, go get him," the older one demanded and the other disappeared.

"I've gone insane," Hailey whispered, and the older maid snorted.

"Not likely, though one look at that dreamy demon face certainly had my mind in a titter. I'm much too old for a young buck like him, however."

Hailey was speechless. Her mind tried to wrap around what she was seeing and hearing and what she thought she remembered, but every time she tried to justify it, she came up empty. How could she be seeing ghosts? And had there really been a horned man who—the ghost maid was correct—was sexy as all hell.

"Maybe the grief finally became too much, and I've snapped," Hailey mumbled as she swung her legs over the side of the bed. She half expected to see her grandmother make a ghostly appearance next, that would make more sense to her. Why was she hallucinating people she didn't know? That seemed very unhelpful.

As she tried to reason through it all, the door opened and in walked the horned man himself. His hood still down and with the backlight of the hallway shadowing his face, he looked like the most intimidating of nightmares. Hailey pulled her feet up off the floor and gripped the comforter.

She decided that if this wasn't a dream or a psychotic breakdown, she needed to start getting some answers sooner rather than later. "Who the hell are you?" she demanded with less shake in her voice than she would have expected for the way her insides were turning.

He walked in further and turned on a lamp by the bed, filling the room with a low light. His face was still a bit shadowy but now she could at least see his features; handsome and dangerous in a way that she found ridiculously attractive. If she'd seen him in a bar, she would have bought him a drink and challenged him to a game of pool or darts. Then she would have agreed to go home with him even though it was probably a terrible idea. She'd have called her grandmother the next day and given his name, gotten the dirt on whether or not to agree to a date if the guy even bothered to call.

"My name is Vint D'red and you are Hailey Silver. Your grandmother was Merry Honeycomb-Silver."

Hailey nodded, her mind reeling at his name. *Vint!* As in, the guy whose name was scratched into her underwear drawer? The mysterious name she'd used for every fake boyfriend fantasy she'd ever created since she was old enough to have those kinds of desires. Hailey looked at him, mouth gaping and unable to form a coherent thought. He knew who she was, what did that mean, and why, if he knew her, did her grandmother never tell her about him?

It could only mean that this man was bad news, the kind that Merry would have warned her to stay away from.

Vint waited and watched her as these thoughts tumbled around her scattered mind. He looked irritated and when she didn't say anything he huffed and asked. "How much do you know?"

What kind of question was that? "I don't know," she snapped. "Why don't you ask me how many fucking stars are in the sky? If I knew what I didn't know, I'd know it, wouldn't I? Asshole," she mumbled the last.

A half smile lifted his lips and gave the impression that he was mocking her.

She found it far too attractive.

The younger ghostly maid appeared beside the bed then. "She don't know a thing, Sir. The Mrs. said we weren't allowed to show ourselves to the granddaughters on account of the oath." The young maid curtsied and disappeared after dropping that bomb that had Hailey further questioning her sanity.

"Great," Vint grumbled. "Though it's what I expected, I don't have time to explain the rules of the world to you, Hailey. So I need you to just stay out of my way."

Hailey was not one to take orders, especially not from some know-it-all male, so she immediately bristled against his demands and forgot her fear. "What the fuck, dude? This is my house, why are you here? How did you know my grandmother?"

"No, it's not your house, which is part of the problem. It *was* Merry's house, now it belongs to no one."

"I don't think that's how it works. There is a will and there's legal things ..." she trailed off, not really sure she knew what she was talking about. The ghost was right, she didn't know anything, apparently. "What are you?" she demanded finally, deciding that was a more pressing issue.

He ignored her question. "Have you seen the will?"

"No," Hailey admitted. "The lawyer is coming tomorrow."

He nodded. "Have you signed any paperwork that would put the house into your name, make you the owner?"

"No," she gritted, what the hell was this guy after? Was he trying to take over the house like a fucking squatter?

"Then technically you aren't the owner. No one is and that's the problem. It's in-between and when things are in-between, they can be manipulated, stolen."

"So you *are* trying to take the house, you're a thief, or a robber, or ... a con artist?" she ended, unsure that anything she said fit this situation.

Vint just shook his head and rolled his eyes. "No, I am none of those things."

Hailey threw up her hands in frustration. "Then what the hell is going on? I don't understand," she huffed.

"I know, and that's the problem. If you can just go somewhere else, you'll be safe and happy and never have to worry about this shit again, okay? Just the way your parents wanted it. Just go home, Hailey."

Hailey bristled against being told what to do by someone else, she was sick of it. He was looking at her like he expected her to listen, too, as if he knew better and more than her and she was just too delicate to handle whatever the hell this was. She shook her head, "No." She *was* home, no place felt more like home to her despite the years since she'd moved out of her grandmother's home, and she certainly wasn't about to leave at his demand.

"You shouldn't be here," he said, giving her a dark look that sent her anxiety spiking, but she refused to give in to it this time. He was trying to intimidate her and that wasn't fair.

Everything he said seemed to be loaded with meanings that were out of her reach and her head was spinning with the effort to formulate reasonable conclusions. He was no doubt intentionally trying to keep her in the dark, confused and willing to go along with whatever he said. But one thing was for certain, she had no intention of going anywhere. "I am not going home."

"Well then to your sister's place, or a hotel? Boyfriend?" he asked with a sigh of frustration.

Annoyance filled her, pushing the anxiety to the side and she glared at the man. Who the hell was he to tell her to leave this place, her grandmother's home, *her* home. "No," she snapped again. "I don't drive, and I am not paying for an Uber at this time of night to get to the other side of town. Especially since you have no right to ask me to leave."

He raised an eyebrow and swept his gaze over her. "You don't drive?"

That was what he focused on? "None of your business." He didn't deserve an explanation, didn't need to know that she was too nervous, too easily panicked to be safe behind the wheel of a car ever. "And besides, this *is* my home and I'm not letting some psycho with horns kick me out. You've given me no indication of your intentions here and it seems to me that maybe I need to be calling someone to get you out of here, maybe a local priest, that would probably be the smart thing to do."

His mouth lifted in another of his half smiles. "Some psycho with horns?"

She crossed her arms over her chest, daring him to deny the obvious. "Start talking or get out, this is not your house, and I *will* call the police." Something she should have done as soon as she'd woken up but somehow it hadn't occurred to her until now.

He narrowed his eyes at her and she wondered if she'd made a mistake threatening him. She had no idea what he was capable of. Something about him, maybe it was his attitude, the way he stood in the place as if he belonged, had made her think that this wasn't a typical home invasion scenario but something more, domestic maybe. So she didn't want to call the police, didn't feel like it would really help their situation any. That didn't mean she wasn't going to threaten it. She needed some answers.

He let out a frustrated huff. "Fine, if you won't leave, you need to listen to me carefully," he finally said.

She relaxed, and the knot of anxiety in her stomach lessened. She made a motion for him to get on with it.

He pulled a chair away from the wall and sat, legs spread and elbows on the arms of the chair. With his fingers steepled he looked like a delightful devil, someone dangerous in a bad boy way she was usually far too attracted to. Now was no different. She moved on the bed, pulling her legs under her body and wished she was wearing something more *her* and less funeral-appropriate.

She chastised herself for the thought, she shouldn't care what he thought of her, she shouldn't be wishing she was looking sexy, or wondering if he had any other extra appendages aside from the horns.

Like a tail!

Oh fuck, why was that thought so hot? She bit her lip and tried to concentrate on what he was saying as her body heated with possibilities.

"Your grandmother was a witch," he finally said.

"Rude," she snapped.

He shook his head. "No, not like she was mean. She was a real, magical, witch. She practiced the craft, she used to be a part of a coven even, all of that stuff."

Her grandmother, a witch? Images of the woman muttering over herbs, offering a cure for any ailment in the form of tea. Somehow it wasn't a stretch to think her grandmother practiced witchcraft. Maybe it was because she'd faced ghosts and a man with horns tonight, but a witch just didn't seem like that big of a stretch. Hailey thought about all the women who had shown up for the wake, were they witches? Had her father known? Was he one too? Could a boy be a witch?

"Am I a witch?" she gasped, unsure if she hoped the answer was yes or no.

"Do you practice magic?" he asked dryly.

"No," she said with a small pout.

"Then no, you are not a witch. A witch is more than just a lineage, it is something you have to embrace, learn, and practice. If you don't use it, you lose it."

"Are you a witch?"

"Half," he said but offered no further explanation. If she were to judge by the horns on his head, she'd be saying his other half was devilish and why did that send a titillating thrill up her spine? What the hell was wrong with her libido tonight, had it really been so long since she'd gotten laid that she was finding this not even completely human man attractive?

That did answer her question about men being witches though and brought her father back to mind. Could he have been a witch like his mother?

She doubted Vint would know the answer to that question, so she went with something more likely. "Why would my grandmother not tell me if she were a witch?" she asked him. Her grandmother had always been honest to a fault. One time Kathy had gotten a haircut that had looked truly terrible, and their grandmother had taken one look at Kathy and told her she looked like she'd stuck her head under a lawn mower. Kathy had cried, but at least she hadn't gone to school before having it fixed. Even miss popular would have had trouble living that one down.

"From what I hear, it was her son's choice. He wanted a normal life for his kids and your grandmother was oath-bound to keep that promise. It's why the ghosts kept away from you too. But now that she's gone, the oath is void and so here they are."

"And here you are," she pointed out.

"No, I am not here because of the stupid oath, it would have only made you not see my ... alternative appendages ... it wouldn't have actually kept me away from you."

Hailey was so confused. "You are saying I could have met others like you before and not known it?"

"Likely yes, when you lived here in the house with Merry especially. I am sure there were others that stopped by, looking normal to you but your grandmother would have known what they really were. A witch sees everything, unless their powers are bound, like yours and your sister's were."

"Creepy," she admitted, shivering a little.

He stiffened slightly, offended perhaps? "Yeah," he said sharply.

"I still don't understand why you're here and why now?"

"With your grandmother gone, there is a lot of magic up for grabs and I am here to make sure it goes to the right place."

"As in, to you?" she accused, back to thinking him some kind of thief.

"Better me than the other options," he snapped.

She didn't know if that was true or not, but she certainly wasn't about to just take his word for it. "Do you have magic now?"

He snapped his fingers, and a little flame sprang up from them.

"Okay ... so why would you want more?"

"It's not about that, it's about keeping it away from dangerous people."

"You seem like the most dangerous person I've seen around here," she pointed out.

"The worst the world has to offer doesn't always wear a sign proclaiming its evil intent, Hailey," he said with a barely disguised *duh* in his tone. "I know you were sheltered, but please tell me you don't take everyone at face value."

Hailey couldn't argue with that, her grandmother had always said similar things about not judging good and evil by the package it was presented in. She tried to grasp all of what he was saying but she knew she was missing things; it was all too much to process. "So where is my grandmother's magic now?"

"It's here, in this house and land, in the things she most valued." He motioned around and Hailey's eyes followed, assessing objects with a new curious eye. Were there magical items in this very room? How could she tell?

"And someone is going to come get it, but you want it first?"

He nodded. "There is already a rumor going out that this place is up for grabs, the coven came through today, yes? They no doubt assessed that the magic is unsettled because you and your sister haven't taken ownership of it."

"And you heard this rumor?"

"No."

"No?"

"Your grandmother called me when she knew she'd likely not survive the illness. She told me what to expect."

"Oh." Hailey couldn't hide the hurt in her voice at that statement. Knowing her grandmother could have talked to her about all this in those last days but hadn't. Had instead called this guy in, if his story was to be believed, which Hailey wasn't a hundred percent on board with yet.

"Why didn't the coven just take the magic if they were here feeling it out?"

"It's not that simple. Some of them still might try, but magic is fickle. It can be trapped and used, but to truly be embraced in a way that a person could use it over and over, it has to choose you as much as you choose it. I'm guessing that none of the coven members have stepped forward saying the magic calls to them because your grandmother hated them all and so her magic took on a similar attitude."

Hailey had a hard time thinking about something as abstract as magic having an opinion on anything. "So you think someone might be interested in trapping it to use as like a one-time battery?" she asked.

"Exactly."

"And you want to stop them, why?"

"Because anyone who wants that kind of battery, as you called it, is someone who is looking to power something dangerous."

She was still confused. "Why do you care? Just so *you* can have that kind of power?"

"No, I care because I promised your grandmother I wouldn't let them take it," he explained, exasperation heavy in his voice.

Hailey crossed her arms and let her gaze run up and down the man or whatever he was, for a minute. He didn't look outwardly dangerous, except maybe to her ability to keep her often-bypassed two date rule before jumping in bed with someone. But just because he was attractive didn't mean he was telling the truth. Attractive people lied too. "Did she say you should have it?"

"No," he gritted.

"That's what I thought," she said, a little smug. But she knew she needed more information from him, so she wasn't going to push to get him to leave, at least not yet. "So you said it matters that I don't technically own the house. Why?"

"Because if you owned the house, you would be able to keep out any who meant you harm, just like your grandmother was able to."

Hailey thought about the front door and her grandmother's

cryptic words. But if they were no longer true, there was no guarantee that Vint wasn't here to harm her. "I think you should leave." She'd get answers some other way.

"No."

"What do you mean, no?"

"Like I said, I have a job to do, I won't leave until it's done." He stood and crossed the room until he was looming over her on the bed. "And if I wasn't here, you'd already be dead."

"Is that a threat?" She embraced anger over the fear he was instilling in her.

"It's just fact, babe. Take a look out the window. I set a perimeter spell as soon as I entered the house, I could feel them close behind me."

Hailey scrambled to get off the bed and to the window. She didn't see anything at first and was about to scoff at herself for falling for such insanity but then there was movement. Among her grandmother's gardens were large figures skulking about, not quite solid but definitely there and definitely giving her the creeps. She wrapped her arms around her body as a chill crept up her spine and she stepped back from the window. She felt panic start to swirl in her belly and her breath came fast.

"What are they?" she whispered, afraid to draw their attention up to the window. She took another small step back and found herself brushing up against a hard and hot body. The tangible reminder that she wasn't alone did a lot to ease the panic back down.

"They are magic-eaters," he said just as quietly as she'd spoken.

His deep voice and hot breath so close to her ear and neck had her quickly replacing her panic with something just as dangerous if she didn't keep it under control.

Desire.

"Some things don't want to collect the magic as a battery or embrace it like it's their own. Some things want to consume it because without eating magic, or magical beings, they will dissipate completely. See how they hover over the garden. Your grandmother used magic in her flowerbeds, they will likely have the whole thing consumed before morning. Unfortunately, I couldn't spell that wide on such short notice and the house was the priority."

Hailey's heart ached at the idea of losing her grandmother's gardens overnight. "Why now, why didn't they come as soon as she passed?"

"Official death may have occurred a few days ago, but the wake is what marks the passing, and it is what opened up her magic. Everyone saying goodbye, letting her go, it's what released her soul into the afterlife and separated her from her magic."

"I'm not magic, so those things wouldn't harm me?" she asked.

"No, they wouldn't harm you. You are a bland human."

"Rude," she said.

He shrugged. "Truth. You could be more, it's why you can see the magic around you. You have a flicker of magic in you, but until you actually embrace it, you are bland enough that they wouldn't bother you if you walked out there."

"Would I be able to get rid of them if I went out there? Scare them off and save the garden?"

"No, and if you let them know you can see them, they might decide you aren't too bland and you could find yourself in serious danger then."

"Great, no magic and yet still spicy enough to entice the monsters."

He laughed, surprising her with the sound. "You are definitely spicy."

"So what am I supposed to do?" she meant more than just

at the moment, but she'd settle for how to handle the next eight to ten hours.

"Since you refuse to leave, and with those guys out there it's probably best you don't, I suggest you get some sleep. I'll be here until the sun comes up."

"Like a vampire?" she asked with an edge of excitement that came from her latest addiction to paranormal romance books.

"No, not like a vampire," he said dryly. "Like a guy who needs to sleep at some point. I'll rest when there's not likely to be an attack but for now, I need to make sure my wards hold and the magic-eaters keep their distance. On the plus side they'll act as a deterrent to anyone else that might have had the idea to stop by tonight. I'll be back later in the day tomorrow. You should consider being gone."

Hailey had no intention of leaving, not without answers and she certainly wasn't about to abandon whatever her grandmother had here to this stranger. "What if I inherit the house tomorrow? The lawyer is coming with the will."

He looked at her thoughtfully. "If you inherit the house, then you will have to decide what to do with the magic it holds." His face turned doubtful. "Are you up for that?"

"I don't know," she admitted.

He nodded and walked to the bedroom door. "I'll be here all night. You can sleep safe, and I'll be back tomorrow afternoon, maybe I'll see you then."

She didn't say anything, just stared at the door that closed behind him then flopped onto the bed and gazed unseeing up at the ceiling, her thoughts running a mile a minute.

Her grandmother was a witch, there was some kind of horned man in the house, and there were magic-eating shadows outside. And ghosts, can't forget the ghosts in the house. She knew she wasn't crazy, despite her anxiety she knew she didn't have delusions, which meant this was real, and somehow the idea that her grandmother was more than a regular human made perfect sense to Hailey, the woman had been amazing.

And tomorrow she was going to be the official owner of the problem, undoubtedly along with her sister.

Thoughts of Kathy and Summer had her biting her lip. Should she call Kathy and warn her? The clock showed it was too late for calls to be polite and she knew Kathy wasn't a night owl. There was no reason to disturb her sleep, there was nothing to be done tonight, if Vint was to be believed. Because he was keeping watch ... she paused, waiting for anxiety to overwhelm her. He said she was in danger, he said to trust him to keep watch while she slept. It was a ridiculous scenario and yet she only had the slightest bit of anxiety over the situation, she believed him, a stranger that wasn't even human, at least not fully.

"Give me a sign grandma, if I'm not supposed to trust him." She waited for something to happen and when nothing did, she accepted that she was making this choice tonight. She was going to trust Vint, whose name was in her underwear drawer, that she'd be safe until morning. Trusting him beyond tonight, that would be something to figure out tomorrow.

Good luck sleeping with all that, she grumbled to herself then headed for the shower.

When she was showered and in her pajamas, she walked to the bedroom window, hoping to not see any shadow monsters hanging around the gardens. She stepped back with a gasp when she looked down and saw Vint there talking to one of the shadow monsters. Was he actually in cahoots with those things? Should she slip down and lock the front door while he was distracted?

From behind the curtain, she peered out and watched him

wave his hands around and a spark of fire erupt from his fingertips, then the shadows all rushed away.

Had he just banished them?

He turned to look up at her window and she jumped back, hoping he hadn't seen her creeping on him like that. She got into bed and waited for sleep.

FOUR

Vint watched the rising sun outside the house and crossed his arms over his chest. He was tired, more tired than he needed to be because he'd used a lot of energy to get rid of the magic-eating shades last night. But when he'd seen the look of sorrow on Hailey's face at the thought of losing the garden he hadn't been able to stop himself from doing it.

A small black cat walked up and rubbed against his leg then shifted, becoming the familiar form of his best friend.

"Batal, I'm glad you're here. I don't think the girl is going to listen to reason and she doesn't know how to keep herself safe." He knew his voice was harsher than it needed to be, but he couldn't help himself. He didn't want any harm to come to Hailey, and she was being absolutely unreasonable in staying here. Did she have no sense of self-preservation?

"You couldn't convince her to leave and let you take all the magic here for yourself?" Batal asked with fake surprise. His green catlike eyes going wide. "Here I thought your abilities to convince the female gender to do whatever you wanted were legendary."

Vint rolled his eyes, he knew how it sounded, but he really

had half expected her to run screaming, what human wouldn't. She wouldn't need to be convinced to leave if she was scared off, problem was, she hadn't been scared, not really. Intrigued, angry, cute as hell, but not terrified after the initial shock. "No, she is stubborn. She had no idea about magic though, that's for sure. She's like a helpless baby mixed up in this but she's convinced she can't leave it to the adults to fix." Vint didn't add that she was also attractive and saucy, and he wanted to go upstairs and peek at her sleeping, as he'd done multiple times during the night, just to make sure she was okay ... after all, he had told her he would make sure she was safe all night so she could sleep. He was just keeping his word.

Batal gave him a sly smile. "I'll be here all day, go rest. Is the sister here too?"

"No, just Hailey, but Kathy is arriving this afternoon along with a lawyer to settle the estate. I am going to try and be back before then. I want to know what *exactly* the will says, it's going to determine what we can do about the others who are no doubt just waiting to come for the magic. I trust you can keep anyone away if they show up this morning to snoop?"

Batal nodded. "I've got this," Batal assured him. "Do you expect your sister?"

Vint shrugged, "Probably, but it's hard to say with her."

A brief look of disappointment passed over Batal's face before he shifted back into his cat self.

Vint believed his friend would watch over Hailey and the house, but he also hesitated to leave. He knew Merry wouldn't want anything to happen to her granddaughters, they were everything to the woman. He told himself that was why he cared so much, he adored and respected Merry, he owed her for all she'd done for him and his sister. It was that loyalty that had him wanting to stick close now, to watch over Hailey.

But if he stayed, he would get no sleep, and he would need

his strength to fight off a coven if they came for the magic tonight.

He left the house reluctantly and frowned at the garden as he passed. It was half destroyed. He hadn't acted soon enough to save it all. He hoped Hailey wouldn't be too disappointed.

"What are you doing here?" an elderly woman asked from outside the gate. She had a small dog on a leash that growled at him as he approached. She was dressed for an early morning walk, but it was far too early to be that innocent a scenario.

Vint could tell immediately that she was a witch, a coven member. It wasn't anything outwardly different about the woman, it was more of a feeling, as if the bits of magic she held were constantly reaching out and feeling the world around her. They prickled at him then curled away, not liking what they found. He flipped his hoodie up over his horns, not that it mattered now. He'd already been spotted and within the hour every coven member in town would know he was here, which could mean they made a move for the magic sooner rather than later. Shit, maybe he shouldn't leave to rest.

Keeping his voice even he responded. "Protecting Merry's magic."

"Not doing a very good job by the looks of that garden," she said with a sniff. "The eaters have already been here. Or is protection not your goal?" she said with a sneer. "Are you hoping to take it yourself? Did that batty old woman actually leave everything to the likes of *you*?"

Vint clenched his jaw knowing that the witches didn't think much of his kind, or anyone who associated with them. He was half demon and all evil in their opinion, but one witch hadn't treated him like shit, and he was determined to repay that kindness.

Vint glared at the woman and was rewarded with a sharp intake of breath. She might be a powerful witch in her own right, but she was still terrified of what he might be able to do to her. "Merry has kin, you know the magic prefers to stay in the family and I am just here to make sure it has the chance she wanted it to. Away from greedy magic grubbers like you."

She gasped at his intended disrespect. "We're watching you, demon," she spat and moved on at a fast pace.

Great, the coven was going to be all over the house and Hailey in no time. He debated going back in, resting in the house perhaps so he could be on alert and deter any unwanted visitors, but he knew he'd never get real rest in that house, not once Hailey was up and around. He'd be far too drawn to her, tempted to interact with her, even if it was just to make her nervous, hear her heart kick up a beat. No, he'd return soon enough, well rested and capable. He trusted Batal to keep an eye out while he was away and alert him if necessary. So he headed into the nearby woods just far enough that no one from the street could see him, and then with a wave of his hand opened the portal to his own home.

Hailey woke up and stared at the ceiling for a while. She couldn't convince herself that it had all been a dream. Partly because somehow it all made sense, her grandmother having magic. It was like the missing puzzle piece sliding into place and now everything clicked.

She knew she should be freaked out, maybe calling a psychiatrist for an evaluation even, but she just felt ... right. Like she finally understood why she had always felt as if the world was hiding something from her. It had been.

She got up and walked to the window. Half of the cherished gardens her grandmother was so proud of were destroyed, turned black overnight as if a frost had hit hard. A harsh frost in late July … not likely. It was proof that the magic-eaters had been out there, further evidence that last night hadn't been a dream or a psychotic breakdown, and it was also proof that Vint had been here and saved a good portion of the garden from complete devastation.

Did it mean she could trust him?

She wouldn't go that far but it did show that he didn't want harm to come to this place and that was something she could like him for. She shuddered to think what might have happened last night if he hadn't been here, if what he said was true, those weird shadow things might have consumed the entire garden then some. There was magic in this house he'd said, in her too.

But here she was and the house as well. The sun was up on a new day and nothing terrible had occurred during the night other than her dreams of him sneaking into her room, climbing into her bed and … yeah, she needed a cup of tea to calm her nerves for a very different reason than usual today.

Hailey dressed in shorts and a pink tank she'd found in one of the drawers last night, then she was ready to make some tea and maybe enjoy the sunroom. She didn't know if Vint was still downstairs, but she told herself it didn't matter, even as she took a few extra minutes to make sure her hair was brushed smooth and put on a little lip gloss and a swipe of mascara, nothing fancy. A girl just wanted to look nice sometimes.

She took her time walking to the kitchen, listening for any sounds of him, a little disappointed when she got to the kitchen and there wasn't a single sign of the attractive male anywhere. She was also on the lookout for any ghostly entities. She thought she caught something in the corner of her eye near the front door but when she turned to look there was nothing there.

"Well, guess it's just me for breakfast," she said aloud and started some water boiling. She had hours before she'd need to deal with the lawyer and whatever news he was bringing, hours before Kathy and Summer would be here. She was going to enjoy her grandmother's space, for what could be the last time, she knew.

She picked up her cell and turned it on as she pulled out a morning tea blend she was fond of. She wasn't surprised to be immediately notified of messages from friends wishing her well and her boss asking if she meant to take more time off just for the death of her grandmother.

Hailey let out an unladylike expletive. *Just*! She threw the phone on the counter. She'd message friends later probably, but her boss could eat shit. The last thing she'd told him was that she'd call him after the wake and let him know when she'd be back. Apparently, he thought that meant hours after, and back to work the next day. If he decided to fire her because of this then that was his deal, she'd find something else, she always did.

Maybe she'd finally find something that really made her feel good. She certainly didn't have a passion for managing people.

When she turned from the stove with her steeping cup of tea, she saw a black cat sitting and staring at her from the middle of the kitchen. She stared back with a frown.

Her grandmother didn't have a pet, but her words were ingrained in Hailey, she never passed a black cat without greeting it. Even a strange one in her grandmother's house, a woman who refused to own an animal of any kind.

"Hey there, kitty. Where did you come from?"

It meowed and walked to her, rubbing itself against her leg. She bent and picked it up, cuddling it close and kissing its soft head. It began to purr so she decided it liked her. "Did Vint let you in? Maybe you're his cat." She wondered for a moment if this was a demon cat but then shook that thought away, that seemed a little ridiculous. More likely it was Vint's familiar, he was half witch after all. Did witches have familiars, was that a real thing? She'd add that to her list of questions she wanted Vint to answer when she saw him next.

"How about some breakfast?" she said to the cat. "I bet there's something left over from yesterday with fish and cream in it for you."

It didn't respond, but it also didn't try to run so she took that as acquiescence. She set it on the counter and pet its head.

"Did you see any hot horned men or ghosts anywhere? Are they avoiding me? Maybe they don't come out during the day." She knew Vint planned to come back today, during the day, but the ghosts, maybe they were a sundown only thing.

"Ma'am did you need something?" the older maid she'd seen last night appeared in front of her.

Hailey let out a little screech and jumped. The cat let out a meow.

"No, I was just wondering if you were around. Umm, what's your name?"

"I am Valerie, and we are always around, Ma'am. If you or the cat man need anything."

Hailey looked at the cat, was it a boy? She'd take the ghost's word for it, seemed rude to check. "We are having breakfast and tea, I'm sure we can handle that, you can ... do whatever it is you do."

The maid curtsied and disappeared.

"I hope they aren't really always just around where I can't see them," she whispered to the cat.

The cat was staring at the spot the woman had stood making Hailey feel like Valerie was indeed still there just out of sight and she shivered. She'd have to be careful what she said.

Hailey hurried past the spot the ghost had stood and opened the refrigerator. She found the tuna casserole she'd seen yesterday and pulled it out then set it on the counter and peeled back the top. She set the cat next to it. "It's all yours. I don't like tuna."

The cat started eating and by the time her tea had steeped sufficiently the cat was sitting cleaning his face, obviously satisfied.

"Let's go find a spot of sun, shall we?" she said and picked him up with one hand, her tea in the other. "You need a name." She carried him and her tea to the sun porch where a comfortable couch sat bathed in sunlight and overlooking the back yard. There were plants all throughout the room and she had a thought that they may need watered but quickly noticed the damp soil in the nearest. Apparently the ghost maids took care of that. Maybe it wasn't so bad having them around, she'd always killed plants, forgot to water them, or over watered them, there didn't seem to be any in between for her.

"How about Charles," she asked the cat as he curled up on her lap. He looked up at her clearly disliking the name. "Okay, too formal, maybe you're more of a fluffy."

The cat extended a claw into her bare leg.

"Ouch! Okay, fine. What about Midnight?"

The cat settled so she decided it was good enough. She stroked his fur and sipped her coffee, looking out at the back yard. Her grandmother had used that space for a small orchard of fruit trees and it backed up to a tall hedge. From where she stood there was no sign of any damage done here by the magic-eaters last night.

She couldn't believe she was thinking those thoughts, then again, she'd just very reasonably accepted that some ghost maids had watered the plants in here so maybe she just had to believe every damn crazy thing she saw.

How was she going to explain any of that to Kathy and Summer though, and did she have to? "I wish Vint was here to give me some answers," she mumbled into her cup.

The cat meowed and she looked down at him.

"You have an opinion on Vint? If you are his, maybe you can tell me if he's trustworthy. I think he's up to something, but he told me things no one else has and I kind of need that now."

The cat jumped off her lap and walked toward the door leading into the house, he paused and looked back at her.

"What is it, Midnight?" She felt like the idiot humans on *Lassie*, as if the animal was actually trying to communicate, it was ridiculous, he probably needed out or wanted more tuna. She got up, telling herself the whole time she was being ridiculous, but at least no one was here to witness it.

Midnight walked through the door when she opened it and then hurried forward, she followed him through the kitchen and down a hall then into her grandmother's small library.

This was one of her favorite rooms in the whole house. It smelled like books and pipe smoke. Her grandmother told her it was a remnant from when Hailey's grandfather had been alive, but when Hailey had gotten older she'd realized her grandmother indulged in a pipe at least once a week. Maybe just to remember her dead husband, Hailey wasn't sure, but it definitely wasn't thirty-year-old leftover smell.

Midnight walked over to a shelf and jumped up on it then pawed at a book there.

"What are you trying to show me?" Hailey asked. Setting down her half empty tea, she grabbed the book and the cat then settled into a leather chair.

The book was bound in red leather and had wildflowers embossed on the front. No title. It was warm under her hands, and she felt her grandmother's presence strongly as she held it. When she opened the cover, she felt a rightness settle over her.

Honeycomb Family Grimoire, it said on the title page.

"What the hell is a grimoire?" she asked Midnight. She was pretty sure the cat rolled his eyes at her.

She opened the book to the middle, assuming she was about to see an intricate history of her grandmother's family, Honeycomb being her maiden name.

"Is this a recipe book?" she asked as she looked down at what looked to be a tea recipe. "Is this what Grandma used to make all her lovely teas she was so famous for?" Not that Hailey had ever seen her look at a recipe as she'd mixed and measured for a customer. No, Merry had memorized everything or gone off a whim, but here it was, all written down for someone else to learn.

"Why didn't she ever share this with me?" Hailey was a little hurt, she would have cherished this at any point, but now, without her grandmother to talk her through it, she felt like she had been given a treasure she could only half use.

But a treasure it still was. Hailey smiled and looked at the cat. "Thank you. Also, how did you know it was there?"

The doorbell rang, startling her. She stood quickly, knocking the cat to the ground and she was thanked with a hiss. "Sorry," she said as she clutched the book in her arms, unwilling to part with it now that she'd found it. The cat just tilted his head as if to say, *Who could that be?*

CHAPTER
FIVE

Hailey left the comfort of the library and the cat followed. It was too early for the lawyer so it was likely just a neighbor or one of her grandmother's customers.

"Madam, it is Mrs. Hilltop."

Hailey startled at the sight of the ghostly servant man standing in front of the unopened door. She wasn't sure she'd ever get used to that.

"Thanks, you can go take a break," she said uneasily.

The old man nodded his head and disappeared.

Hailey looked down to confer with her companion about whether or not Mrs. Hilltop was someone they wanted to talk to, but the cat was nowhere in sight so Hailey opened the door.

Mrs. Hilltop was a frequent visitor here, had been since Hailey could remember. She was old now, as old as Merry had been, which put her in her seventies, but she got around well, always taking her dog for a walk and getting fresh air. Today she was dressed in a pale yellow sundress with too much makeup on for a woman her age. She held out a basket covered in a pink napkin.

"Muffins. I noticed you were still here and thought perhaps you would like some homemade breakfast."

Food, why did everyone want to feed her as if grief was just a hollow pit in the stomach that could be filled rather than a permanent rip in your soul.

"Thank you, Mrs. Hilltop," Hailey said politely, taking the basket. "Would you like to come in? I could whip up some tea."

The woman looked over her head a bit suspiciously before she smiled and agreed. "Tea sounds perfect, but you sit, let me make it."

Hailey shut the door behind the woman and followed her to the kitchen. It was somewhat comforting to have the familiar face here, as if her grandmother was going to walk in at any moment and make Mrs. Hilltop something to soothe an ache in her bad knee or cure her husband's cold. Like it was just any other day.

"You look like you slept okay," Mrs. Hilltop commented.

"Thanks, I think all the exhaustion of preparations finally knocked me out last night. I'm glad that the ceremony is over so we can focus on more practical matters."

Mrs. Hilltop nodded and hummed as she moved around the kitchen as if she knew exactly what to do, of course she did, she had been here a million times before and watched Merry make tea. She got water boiling then pulled out a tin of tea. When she saw the open tuna casserole on the table she frowned and cleaned it up.

Hailey had a shot of guilt, she should have put that away. She didn't like tuna casserole but that didn't mean she needed to let it go bad. Mrs. Hilltop was probably thinking she was the worst kind of wasteful.

Mrs. Hilltop talked about the weather and her dog while she fixed the tea, but when she sat across from Hailey at the table her face turned a bit more serious.

"What happened to the garden?" Mrs. Hilltop asked.

Shit, Hailey had no idea what to say, no idea how to explain it. She took a sip of tea and stared at the table. "Frost?" she said, more of a question than an answer.

Mrs. Hilltop nodded. "Frost. So what is your plan for the magic in this house?"

Hailey choked on the sip of tea she'd just taken and stared at the woman across from her, momentarily unable to speak. Finally she reigned in her scattered thoughts and stumbled out, "I—I don't know what you're talking about."

"Don't sass me, girl. I know what happened outside. I know that half-demon scum, Vint, was here last night, and I can smell a shifter in the house too. You need to make a decision and get out before even worse things come by. They won't all leave you unharmed."

"Make a decision?"

Mrs. Hilltop rolled her eyes. "About the magic! You can't just let it sit, it needs a home, it wants a home, and if it lands in the wrong hands it's going to be a serious problem."

Mrs. Hilltop's words echoed what Vint had said last night and had Hailey on edge. She took out a muffin and bit into it to buy some time to think.

"I don't really understand what all is going on," she finally admitted.

The woman relaxed across from her and smiled softly. "Your mother hated what she called the *Honeycomb Curse*. She refused to let your father practice, made him give up everything to be with her and raise a family. She forced your grandmother into a binding agreement to keep all magic from you and your sister or your grandmother wouldn't have been able to see you two." Mrs. Hilltop shook her head. "It wasn't fair, your father was a very talented witch, but he was so in love with your mother he was willing to give it all up." Her face turned wistful for a moment. "We all do stupid things when we are in love. Your grandmother, when she took on the raising of you two girls, she hid everything, still bound by the oath she'd taken. She wanted to teach you. She always said you and your sister were both so naturally inclined she hoped someday you'd just figure it out and she wouldn't have to break her oath, but she could teach you anyway."

"A loophole," Hailey said with a grin, her grandmother was definitely the type to like a good loophole for any rule.

"Exactly. But she never found one. Now that she's gone, though—the wake—it released her from the oath and her magical shield that had been over you two was lifted. Now you can see what you were never able to before."

"Like the ghosts," she whispered.

Mrs. Hilltop nodded. "Drandy is the butler and the maids, the young one is Sarah and the older maid is Valerie have you met them all?"

Hailey nodded, thankful to have names for them all now.

"And Vint, that sneaky half-demon. You met him last night?"

Hailey nodded.

"You can't trust a demon, even a half one. I am glad he's gone now. Did you banish him?"

"I'm not—I don't—"

Mrs. Hilltop stopped her with a raised hand. "It's fine, I was getting ahead of myself, of course you can't. So here's what we are going to do. I am going to help you send that magic where it was always meant to go. We'll get this all straightened out in no time, and you can move on. No one will be bothering you then."

A prickle of unease crawled up Hailey's spine and a knot of anxiety started to form in her stomach. Something wasn't right. She set down the muffin. "Where exactly is it that you want to send the magic?"

"Why, to the coven of course! Your grandmother was an important member, and we all draw strength from each other, it is why covens exist; to share in magic, and experience, and power so we can all take care of each other. It is what your grandmother would have wanted, and we can take care of it right now, real quick. You already found the grimoire I see." Mrs. Hilltop motioned to the book Hailey had set on the table.

Hailey reached out and pulled the book into her lap. "What is a grimoire, like a recipe book?" she asked, avoiding the question of her grandmother's magic.

"It is a book of spells. That one is a collection of everything the Honeycomb line has ever come up with and because they focused their magic around teas, I'm sure they read like recipes." The woman's eyes were almost greedy as she looked at the book.

"I don't think I am ready to get rid of anything of my family's. I don't think my grandmother would have wanted me to rush to do anything and the lawyer is coming today. We expect her will to spell out exactly what she wanted to happen when she passed."

A brief look of anger passed over Mrs. Hilltop's features before she once again smoothed her face into a placating smile. "The lawyer, yes, of course," Mrs. Hilltop said tightly. "Well, you don't want more unseemly creatures creeping around, like the magic-eaters. Can you even imagine what would happen if someone like Vint gained control of this magic? Not to mention the sneaky shifter." Her eyes darted around the room.

"I have no idea," Hailey said honestly, not even able to concentrate on what Mrs. Hilltop might be implying about a shifter. All she did know was that her anxiety told her Mrs. Hilltop was not on her side and her grandmother had always told her to trust her gut. Nothing else in the house had given her such a raw feeling of wrong, not the ghosts, not Vint, just

Mrs. Hilltop and her greedy presumptions. "I think that I'll know more soon, but you don't need to concern yourself with me, Mrs. Hilltop. I'm an adult and I am sure that Kathy and I will be able to deal with whatever needs to be dealt with here. If that changes, you'll be the first to know." She added the last hoping it would convince the woman to leave without argument.

"I see," Mrs. Hilltop said and stood, clearing the table of her teacup and rinsing it in the sink. "I am going to stop by later because as your grandmother's dear friend it wouldn't be right not to watch after you in this time of transition. After you've had time with the lawyer we'll talk." She paused and looked intensely at Hailey. "It is important that the magic isn't sent to the wrong place you know. You have a duty to take care of it properly, get it to the right people."

Hailey wanted to scoff at the words, so much like what Vint had said but somehow more menacing. "And you are the right people?" Hailey challenged.

Mrs. Hilltop lifted her chin and pursed her lips. "I am not the enemy here, Hailey. You don't understand a thing about magic, it would be dangerous for you to try and pretend you understand this world your grandmother lived in. A world that has always been kept from you. Outsiders don't just walk into magic and know what to do with it, that's why your mother was so against it when she found out what your father and his family were. She was an outsider and she hated everything to do with magic because she didn't understand. You may not hate it, Hailey, but you don't understand, and that's possibly more dangerous." The woman's face softened into something that could almost pass for empathy. "And we all know how anxious you get, poor thing. I wouldn't want you to lose your head over all this trouble."

Hailey stood with the book clutched to her chest. "You may

be right, but I am not going to jump to any decisions that don't feel right. That's not what my grandmother taught me." She was proud of the way she held her voice steady even as the woman's words stung her where she was most vulnerable.

"No, of course not." Mrs. Hilltop gave a bright smile. "I will see you later, I assume you plan to stay here, because if the house is left empty there will be no one to protect it." The seemingly caring words sounded more like a threat.

"Yes," Hailey said firmly even if that hadn't been the plan at all, there was no way she was going to let her grandmother's magic be taken by anyone unless she felt like it was exactly what her grandmother had intended. Nothing about what Mrs. Hilltop had suggested felt right.

"Wonderful," Mrs. Hilltop said and walked out of the kitchen.

Hailey followed and only jumped slightly when she saw Drandy's ghostly form open the door for Mrs. Hilltop. "Have a good day, Mrs. Hilltop," Hailey said.

When the door shut, she slumped against the wall, sliding down to the ground. Midnight came out of the other room and pressed against her side.

"Where were you during that visit? I could have used the cat support."

He just meowed and snuggled his head against her thigh.

Hailey stayed there on the floor petting the cat for a while before she felt completely calm again. Very unsure, but at least not knotted up with anxiety. She opened the book on her lap and started flipping through it again. They were unmistakably tea recipes, herbs and flowers, fruits and spices. But Mrs. Hilltop had said they were spells. So she paid attention to the titles on each one with that in mind. *Calmer, Love Story, Defender*. They could mean anything.

"Maybe there's something here that can help me figure all

this shit out. Something to make me understand or ensure I make a good decision," she mumbled as she flipped through pages.

Midnight had fallen asleep next to her and so she didn't move, just kept looking through the recipes.

A quarter of the way through the book she stopped at a page that was titled. *The Third Eye.* She read the recipe and it sounded familiar. She was sure she'd seen her grandmother make it. It had orange and cinnamon in it and she loved a spicy sweet tea.

"The third eye is all about knowledge and self-awareness," she said to herself. "Perhaps that's exactly what I need right now."

She looked at the clock, there was still a while before she'd be likely to see Kathy or Summer, so she decided to give herself some clarity. She woke Midnight as she got up and walked to the kitchen. He sleepily followed, jumping up on the counter when she set the book down and staring at the page as if he were reading it.

"This sounds good, right? Maybe it will help me figure out what to do."

The cat sat and looked at her with a cocked head.

"No opinion on the matter?" she asked, then went about searching for the ingredients. She pulled out the dried orange peel, the cinnamon and the black tea leaves. The recipe called for green, but she preferred black.

She filled a small tea ball just as she'd seen her grandmother do a hundred times and reheated some water. Midnight was once again sleeping, having settled into a spot of sunshine on the counter, as she poured the hot water over the ball and the aroma filled the air.

Hailey leaned over and inhaled the warm scent, letting it fill her senses as it steeped. Then she ran her finger over the last line, one she'd seen on many of the recipes.

To truly get the benefits one must think on their reasons as they sip.

Think on her reasons. Well, she was looking for insight, for clarity and to know the difference between good and evil. She wanted to know what the right thing to do with her grandmother's magic was. She repeated that in her mind and under her breath twice then sipped the hot tea. She closed her eyes and felt it warm her as her words of intent swirled through her mind.

"What the hell am I doing in this godforsaken place again?"

Hailey screamed and turned to find herself face to face with something truly terrifying. He was massive, at least seven feet tall and so wide he would likely have to go sideways through any doorway. His deep red skin glistened, long black horns curled menacingly from his forehead. His mouth was distorted by fangs protruding between black lips and his eyes glowed a bright white. His legs bulged in an odd way that had her eyes going down to take in his hoofed feet. A swish behind the beast had her assuming he had a tail back there and she really didn't want to confirm that.

She screamed.

Out of the corner of her eye she saw Midnight transform instantaneously into a short man with skin as black as night and large green catlike eyes. He was still sitting on the counter, but he held a small knife out, pointed at the beast that had spoken behind her.

"Get out!" Midnight hissed at the beast.

"What the fuck!" Hailey yelled, unsure if she had accidentally dropped acid with her tea.

The back door opened and in stepped Vint looking like he was ready to attack whatever he found inside.

SIX

Vint had been on his way back when he'd felt a couple things, first was the use of magic. Hailey was casting a spell which was dangerous considering she was untrained. And the other, a shift between realms that meant a demon was about to pop up nearby. He'd been worried, but then he heard her scream, and he was terrified. He ran the rest of the way to the house and burst into the kitchen.

His gaze sought out Hailey, she appeared whole and unharmed, but wide-eyed and clutching a teacup like her life depended on it. He moved quickly and took in the rest of the room. Batal was crouched on the counter in his human form glaring at an unwelcome demon.

"What the fuck, why did you summon my father?" Vint demanded. Of all the demons that she could have summoned, why this one? Why Grail D'red? Vint crossed his arms over his chest and took a step closer to Hailey, ready to jump into action if an attack was imminent. His protective instincts were on high alert and by the slight interest that widened his father's eyes briefly, he knew that the action wasn't missed.

Hailey turned to Vint. "Father?" she squeaked.

"Yeah, why the hell did you summon him?" Vint snarled. This man was dangerous and if he thought that Hailey was important to Vint, he'd destroy her for the fun of watching his son suffer.

Hailey shook her head nervously. "I—I didn't, I was just, just, making tea, I—"

Vint snapped his gaze to Batal and hissed, cutting off her stumbling words. Vint was supposed to keep her from doing anything stupid or dangerous, this constituted both.

Batal held up his hands and took a small step back. "She changed the recipe, Vint. I swear I dozed for like two seconds and she didn't follow the damn thing. It would have been harmless," Batal defended as Vint continued to glare at him. "You did change the recipe, it wasn't my fault," Batal said, turning to Hailey with a look of betrayal.

Hailey swayed a bit on her feet as if she were about to pass out from the shock of it all. "Midnight?" she whispered, looking at Batal.

Batal gave a bashful smile. "Actually, it's Batal, but I figured Midnight was better than the other options you had for my name," he said with a wink that irritated Vint.

"Oh my god, you're a cat," she whispered.

She was clearly freaking out and Vint was worried she might completely lose it. Vint could see it written across her features and in the way her fingers clasped the cup. He wanted to reach out and comfort her, but his gaze flicked to Grail and saw him watching them too closely.

"No, I am a shifter," Batal explained. "I am a man, but I take a cat form when it suits me."

"I cuddled with you!" she accused.

Vint couldn't hide the glare he shot at Batal. What had the sneaky bastard done while posing as a normal cat?

Batal gave her another lopsided grin. "Yeah, you are a great cuddler."

"Why am I here? Merry doesn't like me much anymore," Grail snarled, keeping Vint from lashing out at his friend. "Vint, I am going to eat you like I should have done when you first popped out of your mother."

Vint wanted to roll his eyes at the familiar threat. Not that his father couldn't make good on it, he just never had. It was likely because Grail rather enjoyed torturing him and if Vint were dead, Grail couldn't any longer.

"Woah!" Hailey said, holding up her hands. Apparently the threat of his death was enough to break her out of her nervous stupor. "Everyone calm down, no one is eating anyone." She turned to look at Vint. "This was an accident. I was thinking about clarity and knowledge. I wanted help making decisions. I never asked for a fucking ... whatever he is."

"He's a demon, obviously. The demon Grail D'red, my father," Vint explained with clenched teeth.

"How do I get rid of him?" she asked desperately.

"You need me," Grail said quickly. "I wouldn't be here if you didn't. What is it that you needed help with? What were you seeking when you drank the tea?"

Vint glared at his father.

"No, no way." Hailey shook her head in denial and set her cup down finally and rubbed her palms on her shorts as if they were sweaty from nerves.

Vint wanted to comfort her, help her, but there were unbreakable laws when a demon was summoned.

Grail smiled at her and even though it wasn't outwardly vicious, it was full of sharp teeth and no doubt not a comforting sight to Hailey. "You made summoning tea and thought about what you need, I am here to provide," Grail explained.

"I didn't mean to," she squeaked.

Vint couldn't stop himself from reaching out to her then

and laid a hand on her shoulder in comfort. He hated the way she automatically stiffened and darted her gaze to him as if she expected to be attacked from all angles. He gave her a slight nod and squeeze. He hoped it was reassuring that he knew she hadn't done this intentionally.

"You were supposed to use orange essence, not dried orange peel for Third Eye Tea, and you were supposed to use green tea leaves, you put in black." Batal was sniffing her cup with a frown. "You can't just go around changing recipes, you have magic in you, it matters what you do and what you intend, Hailey," Batal chastised.

"And you were supposed to keep her from doing anything stupid like this until I returned," Vint snapped at Batal.

"Cats nap; it's what we do," he defended. "And besides, if she'd followed it right, she would have been fine."

"Okay, I messed up, but I still don't understand how he's supposed to help me," Hailey said, motioning to Grail.

Grail shrugged. "Tell me the issue and maybe I can tell you. Were you wanting to know if Vint is worth the hazard to date? No, he's not."

"Don't tell him a damn thing, he does nothing but trick, demons can't be trusted," Vint snarled.

"*You're* a demon!" she snapped back.

"Half," Vint gritted.

"Barely a demon," Grail grunted, crossing his arms over his massive chest. "Just a wee runt, mostly witch like his mother. He doesn't even have another form, and no tail."

Vint ignored the familiar list of his shortcomings. His mother had managed to hide him for the first five years of his life, otherwise Grail probably would have actually eaten him. He wasn't exactly sure why the demon hadn't then, Grail certainly threatened it every time their paths crossed.

"Wait," Hailey said, slowly turning to fully face Vint and

breaking the hold he'd had on her shoulder. "Are you my uncle?" she gasped, staring open mouthed at Vint.

"I assure you we are *not* related," Vint said, he didn't add *thankfully*, but he felt it and the grin on Grail's face demonstrated he knew exactly what Vint was thinking.

"Merry was a looker in her youth though, so I wouldn't have fought her off if she'd been into it," Grail said. "Where is the old woman anyway? I haven't seen Merry in ages."

Hailey bit her lip and turned back to Grail. Grail looked at her and for just a moment, his features softened. Vint couldn't be sure, the look was so fleeting, but it wasn't a look he'd ever seen cross Grail's face before.

"I see, she's passed and so her magic is going a bit restless and you're in charge of deciding what to do with it?" Grail guessed.

"I don't know what to do," Hailey whispered.

"And that's why I am here," Grail said with a grin. "To help you decide where all this goes?"

"No, you are an accidental summon, now you need to leave," Vint said firmly. There had to be some kind of loophole here they could use to send him away immediately, like a misdialed phone number; just hang up and try again.

Grail met Vint's eyes and his flashed with fire, his grin wide. "You know it doesn't work that way. I can't leave until whatever the summoner needs has been satisfied. So it looks like I'm here until she decides what to do with the magic."

"Aren't you supposed to help, then, give me clarity?" Hailey said with a bit of hope that Vint knew was misplaced, Grail would never be of help in this situation.

Grail shrugged. "I could, but why on earth would I shorten my stay on this side?"

And there was the truth, Vint thought.

"Asshole," Batal hissed.

"You can't trust a demon," Vint said. "But he's right, Hailey. He won't leave until the magic is settled if that's what you were thinking you needed help with when you summoned him."

"I didn't summon him," she gritted but she couldn't deny his presence and she had obviously changed the recipe.

"Accidents happen," Batal offered with a soothing tone. "The important thing is what we do after them. So maybe we take care of this magic thing before Grail is let loose on the town."

Vint wanted to agree, wanted to use this situation to push his own agenda, get her to give him the magic. And he hated himself for it.

Hailey threw her hands up in exasperation. "It's not up to me. I'm sure Grandma had a plan. We are going to be reading the will in—" she looked at the clock, "—an hour. And my sister and her fiancée will be here any minute. You all need to leave. I don't think they would take your presence very well."

"If she's your sister, she's going to be feeling the power too. You can't hide it from her," Vint pointed out.

"Well, what about her fiancée? And the lawyer, too?" Hailey said. "I assume Grail doesn't just go waltzing around in front of regular people. I think you all need to leave."

Grail rolled his eyes and snapped his fingers. Suddenly he looked like a human, well, a human who got paid to kill people. He was still enormous, still looked angry and was covered in tattoos. But the tail and horns were gone, he had a head of thick black hair and there was nothing outwardly supernatural about him. But a witch would know, it was likely that even Kathy would be able to see there was something unnerving and different about the large man, and Vint too. But there was no way Vint was leaving this house, look what had happened when he'd left for a few hours. Hailey needed him and he wanted to stay close to the magic.

"Cool trick, but what am I supposed to say? Hey, Sis, here's my new boyfriend Grail and don't worry that he looks like he eats babies, he's just going to sit in on this little reading of the will," Hailey huffed.

Grail laughed.

Vint touched Hailey's arm, gaining her attention. "Look, Hailey. I am not going anywhere, I owe your grandmother and I will repay her by keeping you safe, especially from him." Vint jabbed a finger in Grail's direction. "But really, you are just going to have to let your sister see and understand, her fiancée too. There are plenty of people who know about magic and demons and shifters, even if they don't have a connection to the magic aside from who they love. Everything will be fine after they settle into the knowledge like you did."

Hailey looked doubtful, but she didn't argue. "Okay, but everyone hides until the lawyer leaves," she snapped. "Poor guy would probably have a heart attack if he saw you three for what you are, and I can't explain anything to my sister in front of him."

Batal turned back into a cat and sat at her feet, meowing up at her sweetly.

"My grandmother didn't have a cat; you'll need to stay hidden too."

Batal nodded his feline head.

Hailey shook her head. "I can't believe I fell for your little act."

"Don't feel bad, it's very difficult to tell the difference if you aren't expecting it," Vint said.

"That witch Mrs. Hilltop knew. She said there was a shifter in the house," Hailey grumbled.

"You let someone in the house?" Vint snarled and glared down at Batal who just sat and started to lick his paw. What a worthless guard cat he'd turned out to be.

"She's been here a million times, used to buy teas from my grandmother, it's not like I let in a stranger. Besides, her and most of the town waltzed through yesterday."

"Your grandmother may have sold them teas, but she didn't associate with the coven, and they are only after the magic. They don't care about you, or what Merry would have actually wanted."

"I know," Hailey said. "And I already told her that I am not making any decisions that I know my grandmother wouldn't approve of. The lawyer is coming soon, nothing needs to be decided before that."

"I'm sure she took that well," Vint said.

"About as well as a cup full of vinegar, but she left, no harm done."

"No harm? I doubt that," Grail said. "Those coven witches are trickier than a demon when they want to be, did she bring anything in or go anywhere you didn't see?"

Hailey frowned. "She brought me some muffins and we had a cup of tea."

Vint walked over to the basket that still held muffins and sniffed it. "I don't smell a spell."

"Maybe she was just after information, what exactly did you tell her?" Grail asked.

"That I wasn't making any decisions yet and I wasn't going to let the magic go anywhere that my grandmother wouldn't have approved of."

Vint threw the basket of muffins in the trash. "Next time don't let them in and you sure as hell shouldn't eat anything a witch hands you; haven't you read any fairy tales?"

Hailey's cheeks turned red; she really should have thought twice before accepting what Mrs. Hilltop had been offering.

They all froze at the sound of a car coming down the

driveway. "Go, all of you out," Hailey said in a high anxious tone.

"We'll be upstairs," Vint said.

"Wonderful," she said and hurried to the front door.

Hailey wasn't sure what she was going to say to her sister or Summer, but it was going to have to wait until after the lawyer had come and gone. She paused before opening the door and looked up the stairs. "Hey, no eating your son or whatever up there, Grail. No eating anyone."

She heard a dark laugh in response, and she had to just hope that he had to somewhat abide by appropriate rules of society while here, or at least abide by the wishes of the one who had summoned him.

How the hell was she even thinking such insanity? She'd summoned a demon? It was unreal.

Almost as unreal as the half-dead garden the magic-eaters had destroyed and the cat that shifted to a person … and somehow the fact that knowing her grandmother was a witch made a whole hell of a lot of sense.

She hoped Kathy and Summer would take it well.

"No ghosts," she hissed before opening the door and hoped they would listen.

"Hailey," Kathy said with a sigh as she embraced her sister. Summer was right behind with a look of concern on her face.

"I'm fine," Hailey said with a roll of her eyes. They treated her like she was barely capable of taking care of herself.

Kathy frowned at Hailey and gripped her upper arms. Kathy's gaze bored into Hailey's, searching for any sign of distress. "Are you? Alone in this big house all night, did you even sleep?"

"I slept well, actually. Are you trying to say I look like shit?"

She smoothed her hair and frowned. She knew she wasn't looking super fresh but she thought she was passable.

"You look fine," Summer said quickly. "What the hell happened to the yard?"

"Frost," she said and turned to walk inside. She glared at the slight apparition as they entered the house and it quickly disappeared. Now was not the time to introduce the magical elements of the place.

"We brought some lunch." Summer held up a bag from a deli near where they worked.

"Oh good, all I've had today is a few bites of muffin."

"You made muffins?" Kathy said in surprise.

"No, there was a visitor this morning. You remember Mrs. Hilltop?"

"I swear I saw her yesterday. Why would she come again?" Kathy said.

"She noticed I was here. I think she just wanted to be nice." Hailey led them into the kitchen and snatched up the book she'd left open, shoving it discreetly in a cabinet as she pulled out plates. The herbs and tea mess had been cleared; the ghost maids must have been in here. She couldn't complain about that.

"How about I make us all some tea?" Summer said. "Your grandmother's tea is so special, can't find anything like it anywhere else."

"More true than you know," Hailey said under her breath. "I'll make it," she said louder and set to boiling water and grabbed out a premixed blend, she wasn't taking any chances. "How about something light, a little green tea with lemon?"

"Sounds perfect for lunch," Kathy agreed.

Summer and Kathy plated sandwiches at the table while Hailey stared at the seemingly harmless leaves and herbs in the canister. What would it really do? What if she thought about something accidentally and she sipped the tea and suddenly the world around her exploded?

Her chest tightened and she felt a panic attack coming. She closed her eyes tight and counted to five.

She had seen her grandmother drink this tea a million times and never had anything weird happened, it was likely just tea, nothing more. Even the label declared it was *Green tea with Lemon rind,* nothing special, no cryptic title like *Death To All Earthlings*—okay that would be a pretty obvious title but still.

The kettle whistled and she poured it in a pot with the tea and set the lid on to let it steep. She brought it gently to the table, and then cups, trying to keep her mind from racing toward disaster as she joined her sister and Summer at the table.

"Are you okay?" Kathy asked, laying a hand on Hailey's forehead. "You really don't look well, are you coming down with something?"

"I think I'm just nervous about the lawyer."

"Nervous? What could you be nervous about? We already know what it's likely to say," Kathy scoffed.

"I know, it's just all so final I guess. Nervous isn't the right word for what I'm feeling about today, anxious perhaps."

Kathy nodded understanding and pulled her sister into a side hug. "You're not alone, we are in this together and we will move on from it when it's time. No matter what it says, we don't have to rush and do anything, you know."

Hailey met Summer's gaze across the table and saw some doubt lingering there. Summer didn't think waiting was a good idea; she had been of the opinion from the start that they needed to close up this estate as soon as possible, that it would be a drain on everyone to try and keep it up and move slowly. There would be inheritance taxes and property taxes if they didn't just clear it out and sell.

But Summer wasn't emotionally invested in the place, so it was easy for her to say let it all go. And now it all seemed even more complicated, although neither Summer nor Kathy knew that part yet.

They ate mostly in silence. Summer tried to fill it at first with chatter about the shop but no one else responded much and so it fell to silence as they ate. When Summer poured the tea for everyone Hailey could only stare at it, afraid to accidentally end the world.

"Do you want some honey?" Kathy offered, handing her the little pot shaped like a teddy bear, but Hailey shook her head, afraid of changing the recipe in any way. With shaky hands she lifted the cup and took a sip, trying to think of absolutely nothing as she did. Then she set it down and waited for something horrid to appear.

"You look like you're about to pass out, Summer can you grab some water," Kathy said and started to use her empty plate to waft air in Hailey's direction.

"I'm fine." Hailey pushed her sister away. "Let's get ready for Mr. Webber."

Hailey stood with her plate but Summer grabbed it and shoved a glass of water at her then told her to go sit down and rest. Hailey huffed and left the room, hearing them whisper behind her. They both thought she was too delicate to handle this situation and it was really starting to irritate her. Yes, she was prone to anxiety. Yes, she had moments of panic, but she wasn't a child and she didn't need to be handled like one.

She hadn't even passed out when a demon appeared in the kitchen and a cat turned into a man. But she couldn't exactly tell them that now, it would definitely make things worse.

Too keyed up to relax, she left her water cup on the coffee table and went upstairs to check on the unwanted guests.

It didn't take long to find them, they were hissing and

snarling in a guest bedroom. Hailey opened the door and found Grail on one side of the room, Vint on the other and Batal in the middle with hands spread and a sort of yellow glow coming from his palms pointed at each demon.

"What the fuck is going on? I said no killing each other," Hailey snapped quietly.

"No, you said I couldn't eat him," Grail pointed out and bared his teeth at his son.

Hailey crossed her arms over her chest and glared at the big demon man. "Just sit, chill, do you know what that means? Mr. Webber, the lawyer, is going to be here any minute and I feel like I'm about to accidentally explode the world, so I just need you all to relax so I have one less thing to stress over."

Vint gave her a sympathetic look. "You aren't about to explode the world, or yourself, you're understandably stressed and grieving. Just go take care of things downstairs, we'll be fine up here. He can't actually do anything you specifically tell him not to do since you're the one who summoned him. If he breaks his word to you, he's immediately sucked back to the demon realm."

"Great but still, I accidently summoned him, how the hell do I know I am not going to accidentally do something worse?" she said with a whine that she was far too stressed to care about hiding.

"Can't do much worse than him," Batal said mildly, pointing his thumb at Grail.

Grail smirked, obviously taking it as a compliment. "I won't kill them if that's your wish."

"Don't *hurt* them either," she said firmly. "Just sit and wait, okay. I don't think this will take long."

The doorbell gonged right on cue. "Remember, no fighting of any kind, no killing or anything," she ordered with a finger point to each one until they nodded agreement to her terms.

"Madam, your guest has arrived," Drandy said, appearing in the doorway.

"And you!" Hailey said pointing at Drandy. "You all need to stay well out of sight, *fuck*. I can't wait for this day to be over."

Drandy sniffed disapprovingly and disappeared.

"He's only doing his job, Hailey," Vint chastised, and she glared at him.

"Shut it, Demon Spawn," Hailey snapped in misplaced anger.

Grail and Batal both laughed as she turned and left the room, shutting the door behind her and hoping like hell that no one had heard that conversation. She also hoped Vint wasn't hurt by her comment, but she'd have to worry about that later. She could hear Kathy talking to Mr. Webber already.

SEVEN

"And here is my sister," Kathy said as Hailey came down the stairs. "Hailey, this is Mr. Webber, Grandmother's lawyer."

"Yes, we met when he came before she passed," Hailey said and shook the man's hand. "It's nice to see you again."

Mr. Webber was the epitome of small-town lawyer. He was short, wearing a tweed jacket and had glasses on a round face, a balding head, and an old briefcase clutched under his arm. "And you, I'm sorry it couldn't be under better circumstances."

Hailey smiled politely and they walked into the living room where Summer offered to make tea.

"No!" Hailey said before she could stop herself, gaining the attention of everyone in the room. "I mean, um, please, let me."

"Don't be ridiculous, you have a job to do here, I don't," Summer said and left the room.

Kathy eyed her suspiciously as Mr. Webber started pulling things out of his briefcase. Hailey avoided meeting her gaze, but Hailey couldn't hide the way she was twisting her fingers and tapping her foot. Her anxiety was high. What kind of magical accident was going to come from whatever kind of tea Summer decided to make?

Mr. Webber cleared his throat as he closed his briefcase. "Your grandmother made no changes when I came to see her last week, just so you both know. She wanted to make sure that I had everything in order, but nothing was changed in her last days so there is no contesting this will and saying she was out of her right mind when she made it."

Hailey hadn't even considered such a thing, but it was comforting to know that whatever her grandmother had decided to do with her home and belongings, it had been a decision made a long time ago with lots of time to consider the right options. She looked at her sister who gave a small smile, obviously feeling the same. Hailey grabbed Kathy's hand and they looked at the lawyer. This was it and there was a calmness that settled over Hailey as she waited because it was out of her hands and there was no more waiting.

"I am going to make this as quick as possible; it really is a very simple ordeal and we will need a few signatures at the end. Summer can stand as witness if that is acceptable to you both."

They both nodded.

"Okay, then let's get started." He opened a file then began to read. "I, Merry Antoinette Honeycomb-Silver of sound mind do hereby declare my last will and testament. I leave all my earthly belongings, money, and property to my granddaughters in equal measure to do with as they see most fit."

That was expected.

Mr. Webber paused and looked up, clearing his throat. His cheeks tinted a bit pink and Hailey's stomach clenched with nerves, whatever the next part was, he wasn't excited to be sharing it.

Summer walked in then with the tea service and they all were distracted for a moment as they accepted a cup. Hailey was so caught up in worrying about what the next part of the will said that she forgot to be nervous about drinking the tea until she was a few sips into the minty brew and Mr. Webber was complimenting the blend.

"Well, we all know anything Merry made is good, this smelled divine though, sort of floral and minty, I thought it would be the right kind of refreshing for this occasion," Summer explained.

Kathy gave Summer a quick kiss and patted the seat beside her.

"It is nice, reminds me of sitting with Grandma on a rainy day," Kathy said and as she took the next sip, a patter of rain began to pelt the house.

"Shit," Hailey cursed under her breath and set the cup down. Had Kathy just brought that rain on? "So what's the next part?" she urged, she needed to tell Kathy what was going on before she thought up something worse than a little rain.

"This next part, well, maybe it will make sense to you two because it really baffled me," Mr. Webber said with a slight shake of his head. "But your grandmother insisted it be included ... though technically I don't think it's anything the law could enforce in any manner."

Hailey had a feeling this was it, the decision she and Vint had been waiting for. She sat forward eagerly, her hands clenched anxiously, and her heart was beating so loud she wasn't sure she'd be able to hear what the man said next.

"What else is there to divide up, didn't the first statement cover it all?" Kathy asked.

"Yes, as far as the government is concerned, it did," Mr. Webber assured her, then adjusted in his seat uncomfortably. "And just so you two know, and this was something I told your grandmother as well. I won't be including this bit in the official copy I register at the courthouse."

"Was your grandmother some kind of drug kingpin?"

Summer asked with a laugh, obviously trying to ease everyone's tension.

"Well, don't leave us in suspense," Hailey said, frustrated and about to jump out of her skin.

Mr. Webber looked down at the papers he'd shuffled in his hands and began to read again. "I bequeath my," he paused and cleared his throat again, took a sip of tea and stared hard at the paper in his hand as if he didn't dare meet their gazes. "I bequeath my magic to Vint D'red unless one of my granddaughters decides to step up and claim it, just make sure those hag coven members don't get a drop," he finished in a rush.

"Fuck yeah!" was heard from upstairs and if the shock of Mr. Webber's words wasn't enough, Vint came rushing down the stairs like he'd just won the lottery. He had his hood up covering his horns, but it did little to take the shock of his presence away from everyone in the room aside from Hailey.

"Who the fuck are you?" Summer demanded, standing up and staring at Vint. "Call the police," she snapped at Mr. Webber who pulled out his cell.

"No," Hailey said quickly. "This is Vint D'red, we met earlier."

Summer and Hailey looked at her with shock.

"Great, I'll take his signature on this copy too then. I'll keep this one at my office," Mr. Webber said nervously and opened the file on the table, holding out a pen. "Everyone sign, Summer, you're witness." The poor man looked like he couldn't wait to get out of this crazy situation.

"Hailey," Kathy hissed, grabbing her arm. "How the hell do you know this is Vint, and why is he here and why the fuck didn't you tell us there was someone else in the house? Did he threaten you?"

Out of the corner of her eye she saw Mr. Webber pull his

phone out again as if he'd be on with the police as soon as possible if Hailey said yes. Summer was glaring at Vint and Vint was smiling like an idiot.

"He is who he says he is, no I'm not being threatened, and just sign the damn papers, we'll figure out the rest." Hailey's voice was firm and steady and Kathy looked at her with a bit of shock that sent a spike of annoyance through Hailey.

There was no more discussion as they all signed where Mr. Webber indicated then he gave them each a copy and packed up to leave as quickly as he could.

"I'll be filing this copy with the courts tomorrow. If anything comes up before then let me know."

"Thank you," Hailey and Kathy said as Summer walked him to the door.

Vint stood in the center of the room looking satisfied as fuck. Hailey rolled her eyes at him, and Kathy eyed him suspiciously.

"Okay, what the fuck is going on? Who exactly are you?" Summer demanded when she came back in.

"I am the owner of all this magic," Vint said holding his arms out wide and inhaling.

"Only if one of them doesn't want it." The deep voice of Grail filled the room making all three women's heads swivel to look at him. Thankfully he wasn't in his demon form, but he was still intimidating as fuck and Summer looked like she was about to grab the nearest object to throw at him.

Batal meowed and jumped onto the couch making Kathy scream and jump up which had Summer reacting and grabbing at Kathy to pull her away before she realized it was nothing more than a cat causing the ruckus.

Kathy sighed heavily, one hand on her chest as if her heart were racing. "Grandma didn't have a cat, but hello," Kathy added because they'd both been taught that to not greet a black cat could be detrimental. "Is this yours, Vint?"

"No," Vint said at the same time Batal let out a disgruntled yowl.

"Why don't we all sit down?" Hailey said. "We have some things to discuss."

"Who are these guys?" Kathy demanded. "Really, who the fuck is Vint, and this guy looks like he belongs in prison." She stabbed a finger in Grail's direction.

Grail grinned as if it were a compliment.

"Vint, he's Grandma's ..." Hailey paused because she didn't exactly know. He wasn't Merry's son, that had been a momentary panic earlier, but he had obviously meant something to their grandmother, had even lived here if the name in Hailey's drawer meant anything. Vint just stood silent, not helping at all. "Grail is Vint's father."

"And I'm Batal," he said as he shifted to human form.

"That's one way to let the magical cat out of the bag," Vint mumbled as Kathy and Summer tried to grasp what they'd just seen. Both looking like they were about to pass out, mouths opening and closing in silent gasps for understanding.

Twenty minutes later Hailey had updated Kathy and Summer on everything that had occurred since they'd left the night before.

It was a lot to take in, but things were undeniable after seeing Batal shift into a human and Grail even showed his true form to solidify things.

"So you think the rain is because of me?" Kathy asked, looking skeptically down into her teacup. "Because I thought of it when I drank the tea?"

"What kind of tea did you make, Summer?" Hailey asked.

"It was in a container marked *Memory Wishes*," Summer

said, "I picked it because it smelled good, reminded me of my great aunt who I spent a lot of Sundays with growing up."

Vint nodded at Kathy. "You were thinking of a memory when you drank, a memory of rain?"

Kathy nodded.

"And there you go," Vint gestured outside. "If you didn't have a tendency toward magic nothing would have happened, but obviously you do."

"Yikes," Kathy said and set the tea down. "I think I'm done with that dangerous stuff."

The ghosts appeared then to clear the tea away and although Hailey had described them, seeing them was something different entirely. Kathy and Summer were again rendered pale and speechless.

"I know it's a lot, and I am not really sure I'm not dreaming, but I think this is real, Kath, I think we are magic," Hailey said.

"Okay, so what does that mean?" Kathy said. Suddenly the conversation shifted to what exactly the wording in Grandmother's will meant.

"You don't need to worry about it all. I'm prepared to take it on. I know what I'm doing with magic," Vint pointed out. "This isn't something I'm just discovering."

"You aren't getting the magic unless *they* decide they don't want it," Grail pointed out to Vint again.

Vint snarled at his father.

"Why did Merry even want to give it to you?" Summer asked. "What were you to her, Vint?"

Hailey looked at Vint with curiosity, she'd been wondering the same thing, it just hadn't been a priority to ask personal questions.

Before they had a chance to press him for an answer there was a knock at the door.

"Coven comes a calling," Grail said with a low growl.

Hailey looked at Kathy and she knew her sister was thinking the same thing as her. For whatever reason, their grandmother didn't want the coven to have any part of her magic, and they were determined that they would do whatever they had to do to honor that request.

"Allow me to get rid of them," Vint offered.

"I don't think that's going to work. Mrs. Hilltop didn't seem scared of you when she stopped by earlier," Hailey said.

"Right, a pipsqueak like you could never scare them off," Grail said with a laugh. "I'll take care of this."

"No," Hailey said quickly. "We don't need any trouble. I'll just send whoever it is away. Everyone else stay," she commanded and walked to the door. She didn't think the coven knowing she'd summoned a full demon would do anyone any good.

They grumbled but listened, all but Batal who shifted to cat form and ran ahead of her to perch out of sight of the door on a nearby table. Hailey hated to admit it, but she was thankful to not be facing whoever it was behind the door alone. There was something her grandmother didn't like about the coven, which made Hailey distrust them. Gut instinct told her that the people inside the house right now were the ones on her side, even if they weren't all on the same side as each other.

Hailey opened the door ready to put on a polite but sad smile and send them away, but she was shocked speechless to see a young woman standing there with glowing red eyes and a bright friendly smile. She was wearing a black maxi dress with cap sleeves and a black sunhat. Long red hair flowed down to her waist, and she held a basket in her hands. Looking very much like some sort of dark version of Little Red Riding Hood come to Grandmother's house.

CHAPTER
EIGHT

"Hailey, I presume? I am Gina, Vint's sister and I'm here to make sure that scallywag is behaving himself."

"Gina!" Batal shouted, coming around the door in human form and embracing the small woman. Hailey watched as he stuck his face in her fiery locks and closed his eyes as if blissed out.

Gina squealed in delight and embraced him back, lifting her feet off the ground as he twirled her around the porch. "I thought you were away for the summer, taking a trip south?"

"I was, until I heard the news," she said with a serious tone that didn't seem to fit her girlish face.

"Vint's sister?" Hailey questioned.

"Half, we share a witch mother, different demon fathers. Our mother definitely had a type," she said with a laugh that had Hailey lifting her own lips in a smile. This woman was like a dark ray of sunshine.

"And you're here for your brother?" She wondered if this woman was after the magic too, or perhaps to make sure that Vint got it.

"I knew your grandmother very well, she taught Vint and I

everything we know about magic when our mother died and the covens wouldn't touch us with a ten-foot pole, being half-demon and all, we're outcasts. They are very judgy, I'm sure you've noticed, like mean girls but with the ability to turn you into a toad."

Gina pushed her way into the house with Batal at her side, looking at her like he worshipped the ground she walked on. She was shorter than Hailey but still a bit taller than the small man and he gazed up at her with admiration written across his catlike features.

Gina pulled off her hat and shook her hair out. "So did she do it? Did she leave her magic to Vint? He's so talented. I'm a bit of a bumble when it comes to all that magic stuff, guess I take more after my father," she said with a shrug then smiled slyly. "But that gives me talents Vint doesn't have."

Hailey wasn't sure she wanted to know what talents a demon would have so she didn't ask.

"With stipulations," Vint answered, coming into the foyer followed closely by the others.

"Oh, she always was one to beat around the bush. What, does she want your firstborn?" Gina laughed.

"They have a choice to take it, but if they don't want it, it's mine," Vint explained.

Gina nodded at Vint's words as if they were expected then raised an eyebrow at Grail. "And I suppose you're here to muscle them into acquiescence?" Gina asked Grail. "You finally doing something right for your son?"

"I am here because Hailey summoned me. I am staying until she makes a decision," he said with a smile. "I have no interest in helping Vint get anything."

Gina pursed her lips; the first expression Hailey had seen on her face that could be considered negative. She wasn't sure what to think of this bubbling ball of happiness wrapped in black, but a quick gut check told her there was nothing to fear in Gina's presence.

"I brought cookies." Gina held up the basket. "Don't worry, I didn't bake them. I took them from some woman walking this way right before I sent her in the other direction with a thought of doing something else with her day."

"Coven member no doubt, thanks for helping us avoid that," Summer said, taking the basket. "I am Summer, Kathy's fiancée." Summer held out her hand to the pretty half-demon and they shook hands then Gina reached out to shake with Kathy.

"Nice to meet you both. Now, where are we at in negotiations then? I assume you two are giving it up, right, you weren't taught from birth, you can go back to not knowing, it can all be very easy. It's what your parents wanted after all."

Hailey couldn't tell if Gina really thought that was the best choice or not, the way she said it was vague and almost as if she had no goal other than stirring things up. Which very well could be the case seeing as she was a demon.

Grail stepped in front of Hailey and glared down at Gina. "They are deciding, your brother is not getting something that is wanted by Hailey," he said protectively.

Gina crossed her arms and rolled her eyes. "Got it, you have been summoned to protect, fine. Well then, how about some wine? I know Merry always had a few bottles stashed away for a good occasion. I smelled the cookies by the way, they are spelled to make you sleepy."

Gina left the room with a confident swagger and Batal was right behind her.

Summer cleared her throat. "I'll just see where the wine is and throw these out," she turned and followed as well.

Hailey and Kathy just stared at each other for a minute, unsure what any of this meant. It wasn't what they had ever expected, wasn't what they were prepared to deal with. Hailey felt resentment flow through her; resentment at her parents for keeping this from her and resentment at her grandmother for the same. She quickly pushed that all away though, because they weren't here to explain themselves and she knew that they all loved her and Kathy. Whatever they had decided all those years ago, it was done out of love. Wishing things had been different wouldn't do anyone any good now.

"It's a lot," Kathy said with a sigh.

"Yeah, it is, but we'll figure it out," Hailey said with what she hoped was a confident smile.

Kathy put an arm around Hailey and they walked together into the living room. Kathy took a seat on the couch, Hailey beside her, leaving room for Summer on the other side. Vint chose a chair where he could sit slouched and spread the way a male tends to do when they are trying too hard to look calm. Grail stood with arms crossed leaning against the wall near the cold fireplace. Above the mantel beside him was a large portrait of her grandmother looking regal in her garden, standing among her herbs and flowers in a sundress and hat. The picture had been posed, obviously, taken for this purpose but it was so perfectly her grandmother's personality at the same time that it almost looked like a candid. Hailey had always loved that photo and today as she stared at it she gathered a little bit of strength. That woman was smart, determined, and apparently magical. That woman took everything life threw at her in stride. Two dead husbands, only child dead, raising her grandchildren and apparently teaching two young demon witches too.

"When did you two live here?" Hailey asked.

"We left when your parents passed," Vint said.

"Oh," Hailey suddenly felt guilty. Had them moving in put Vint and Gina out on the street?

Vint shrugged. "We were done with our training, or at least

I was. Gina continued to train a little here and there when your grandmother had time and you two were otherwise occupied."

"Is that why she isn't as talented?" Hailey asked just as the woman, or demon witch, entered with two bottles of wine. Summer and Batal followed with glasses for everyone.

"Wine, your grandmother would have been happy with such a celebration."

"Celebration?" Kathy asked.

"Yes, she always said she wished we could all know each other, and now we have the opportunity. And no, my shortened training is not why my talents are less. I am just not as powerful," she shrugged and opened a bottle while the glasses were passed out. She started to pour for everyone.

Hailey sipped the sweet white wine that Gina had chosen, it was refreshing, and she was thankful for the hit of alcohol as she tried to reason through everything she'd learned in the last day.

"So," Gina said as she settled into the only empty seat and Batal settled at her feet. "What are the ladies of the house thinking?"

Hailey looked at her sister who gave a slight nod. "We will be taking some time, obviously there's a lot to consider here and we don't want to be rash about anything."

"Wonderful choice," Grail said clapping his hands together. "And if I am to be here on the earth side for a while I have a bit of carousing to do." He waltzed toward the door. "Don't make any decisions while I'm gone. I'll see you all before the sun sets and the magic-eaters try to return."

The sound of the front door shutting made Hailey jump. She darted her gaze to Vint who was glaring at her.

What the hell had she just unleashed on Lavender Grove? "Should we stop him?" Hailey asked.

"A little late for that, isn't it," Vint said.

"Well good riddance I say," Gina said and raised her glass. "He's always such a control freak."

"Is he so different from your own demon father?" Hailey asked.

"No, all demons are about the same, tricky and self-involved, you can't trust a word they say, but great in bed."

Hailey choked on the sip of wine she'd just taken. She covered her mouth as wine tried to fly out and she felt her face heat and eyes water as she battled her body's instincts to expel the intrusive liquid from her throat.

"Seriously, Gina?" Vint mumbled.

Kathy patted her back and Summer handed her a napkin. Gina just grinned and took a big drink of her wine, enjoying the chaos her words created.

After that the conversation was carried easily by Gina who talked about her latest trip to South America and how much she hated the jungle. "Far too many bugs," she stated with a shiver and patted Batal on the head. "I could have used you, cats eat bugs, right?"

"Yes, take me with you next time. I will protect you from all the creepy crawlies," he said quickly.

The poor guy was beyond smitten and Gina barely gave him a glance as he stared up at her with wide, hopeful eyes.

"I'm going somewhere drier next. Maybe I'll take a few weeks in Arizona," Gina said with a shrug.

"I love the desert," Batal said but she didn't respond, and he looked away disappointed.

"Would you mind taking me to see her? I'd like to say my final goodbye," Gina asked Hailey. "And since the rain has stopped," she snapped her fingers and the drops faded to nothing, the sun started to shine once more.

If that was not very powerful, Hailey wasn't sure she wanted to know what Vint could do, and why the hell he would want more magic on top of it? "Of course, I don't mind at all, we buried her in the family plot next to our parents, her older brother and both husbands."

"I'll clean up here and then we need to head home and grab a few things. I feel like we should stay here with you until things are settled," Kathy said firmly, giving Hailey a look that clearly said she wouldn't be convinced otherwise.

Hailey smiled at her sister, it would be much more comfortable to not be alone with three demons and a shifter cat and there was no way she'd leave them all here on their own. "Sounds good."

"We can clean it up, Miss," Valerie said appearing out of nowhere.

"Fuck," Summer hissed.

"She can see them too," Gina said with surprise. "Are you a witch, Summer?" Gina asked with a sly smile and leaned forward.

"No, I am certainly not. The most magical thing I can do is make pancakes that are light and fluffy." Summer laughed nervously.

Gina tilted her head, her red eyes narrowing as they eyed Summer speculatively. "You can see my eyes, right?"

Summer nodded. "Who could miss them, they glow like fucking rubies backlit with a flame."

Gina shook her head. "Humans can't see them, they just look brown," she said with a frown. "Dull, dumb brown, and my brother, you see his horns, right?"

Summer nodded.

"I wonder," Gina stood and crossed the room then sat on the table in front of Summer and eyed her like a specimen in a zoo. "What is that," she asked, pointing to Summer's necklace.

"It's one of Kathy's designs," she said giving Kathy a proud smile. "She designs jewelry, and I sell it in my family's store. This is one of her originals."

"May I?" Gina asked and reached out for the charm.

Summer nodded and Gina picked up the small silver charm. It was an intricate design with three black stones set in the middle. It reminded Hailey of stars in a sky, except in reverse where the stars were black and the sky was bright.

Vint had sat forward as his sister moved, interested in what was going on, his sharp eyes focused on the charm as well.

Gina dropped it and smiled at Kathy. "You made your girlfriend a talisman, it is imbued with enough love magic that it reveals all truth to her. Did you know what you were doing when you made it?"

Kathy shook her head, eyes wide. "No I—" she paused and looked at the necklace. "When I made that piece, I felt driven. I wanted to make something for Summer that showed her how much I loved her and how much I appreciated that she accepted me and who I am. She never pushed me to do more than what I wanted, and she just saw me for me, no need to change or improve. From the very start of our relationship, she'd treated me like no one else ever had and I wanted her to know how much that meant to me."

"That, my dear, is a spell. Intention is everything and it has made it so that Summer can see whatever it is you understand as reality. It didn't really activate until now, when the spell that held back what you could see was taken away. You and Hailey are obviously both very natural witches, what with the whole summoning one of the most powerful demons in the demon realm and this powerful talisman. Wow, I wish Merry had been able to see this, she'd be so proud of you both."

Tears sprang to Hailey's eyes, and she put a hand on her sister's thigh as Summer embraced her from the other side. "Our grandmother *was* proud of us, I know that," Hailey said. "I don't think she wanted us to be anything other than what we wanted to be."

"But she would have wanted you to have all the choices, nothing hidden. Which is why she's given you the choice of taking the magic or not, now that she can. She still wants you to have a choice," Gina said.

"How do we even begin?" Hailey mumbled and stood, knocking back the last of the wine in her glass. "I'll get my shoes, you have to drive," she said to Gina.

"Vint will drive," she said happily. "He's good at all that human shit, I never learned."

Hailey smiled at the small woman. "Me either, seems a bit too stressful."

"Especially when you have as short a fuse as Gina does," Vint mumbled and sipped his wine. "I'll drive."

CHAPTER
NINE

Hailey headed upstairs and Kathy followed with a determined look on her face.

"Are you sure about this, you are okay to be alone with those two?" Kathy whispered after shutting the bedroom door behind them.

Hailey grabbed her running shoes and pulled a fresh, albeit unmatching, pair of socks out of the garbage then sat on the bed. "Yeah, I was alone with Vint all last night, the only thing he did was get rid of the magic-eaters before they completely destroyed the gardens." And invaded my dreams in an erotic way she wasn't about to share with her sister. "I don't think he's a bad guy, Kath. There's no way Grandma would have trusted him if he was. You know that."

Kathy crossed her arms over her chest, unable to deny Hailey's point. "It's all, just a lot, you know."

"Yeah, it is and if I hadn't seen so much with my own eyes in the last twelve hours, I wouldn't believe a word of it, but damn." And now they just had to deal with it. This wasn't the first time their lives had been completely turned upside down, likely wouldn't be the last either.

"Fuck," Kathy agreed. "What do you think you want to do, about the magic and all, I mean ... we'd talked about selling the house, this feels like such a bigger decision."

Hailey stared down at her feet intensely as if she had to remember how to tie her shoes. She knew she needed to tell her sister that she didn't want to sell the house, now more than ever it felt wrong.

"Yeah, that's what we'd said," Hailey agreed without commitment and stood. "I'll see you guys back here before sundown. I'll have Vint stop at the grocery store for something to make for dinner, chicken and salad maybe? Anything but casserole would be nice." Not to mention she wasn't sure she trusted any of the food that had been brought to the house by possible coven members, what if it contained a spell hidden inside?

"Sounds good, call me if *anything* happens. I'll run to your place and grab you some changes of clothes. I know you weren't prepared to stay here."

"Thank you and I will," she assured Kathy and walked out of the room. Vint was standing by the front door with his hood up waiting for them. He was shadowed and menacing, well ... he should have been menacing but instead he was undeniably tempting. Hailey's stomach fluttered with something that wasn't anxiety and she bit her lip to stop herself from flashing a smile his way. He wasn't a sexy stranger across the bar, he was some kind of half-demon who was after her grandmother's magic. Feeling things for him in a carnal way would be completely inappropriate.

His dark eyes widened a bit as they focused on her mouth but he quickly looked away as if he were of the same opinion.

"Batal is staying to watch the house. It isn't smart to leave it empty before everything is set and official," Vint said a bit gruffly.

"Oh, that makes sense. Why the hood, if humans can't see the horns?" she asked.

"Makes witches nervous to see them and there are more of them than you'd expect, especially in this town."

"I don't find them intimidating," she said with laugh. "I think they are kind of cute little things."

"Oh! She just called your horns cute little things!" Gina laughed as she came up to them with a refilled glass of wine then turned to Hailey. "That's like insulting his dick with a compliment, not something a demon wants to hear."

Hailey's cheeks turned crimson and Vint glared daggers at his half-sister. "Drinking all the way, huh sis?" he snarled.

"I'm in mourning, I can do what I want," Gina huffed. "You're just jealous because you have to drive." She snapped her fingers and another glass was suddenly in her other hand. She held it out for Hailey. "Cheers, love, you just burned him worse than a trip to the demon realm and that is worth a drink I'd say."

"I didn't mean—" she started, but cut off the words when Vint's glare turned to her. She took the glass Gina offered and shot back half of it. She was going to need the help if she was going to survive this outing. She thought about Vint's father as they walked outside. Grail had really big horns in his demon form, curved back and glimmering on his head. Vint was obviously sensitive about it, but it wasn't his fault he was half witch. She doubted it meant everything was small.

She used her peripheral vision to look him over and tried to decide if it was all shadow or not that was swaying between his legs in those jeans he was wearing.

Fuck, what was wrong with her? She was undressing a half-demon she barely knew with her eyes. She looked down at the now empty cup in her hand. Oh, yeah, day drinking was a dangerous sport.

"Do you need another?" Gina asked, raising her hand to no doubt snap her fingers.

"No!" Hailey said quickly. "But that's a cool party trick."

"One of her only," Vint grunted.

Gina stuck her tongue out at him and put on a pair of dark sunglasses.

"At least no one said my horns are small," Gina said with a smirk.

Hailey wanted the ground to open up and swallow her as Vint stiffened beside her. His truck was parked on the street outside of the yard, a massive black beast lifted up so high she'd need a step to get in, gleaming in the sun like a polished stone. Usually when she saw something like this, she thought the guy was compensating for a small dick, but she assumed this time it was a compensation for the small horns.

As the thought bubbled up in her mind, she couldn't help the giggle coming out, no doubt unleashed because of the wine in her system. She covered her mouth and tried to cough but there was no hiding her laughter from either demon and although Gina found Hailey's inability to hold back amusing, Vint looked like he was ready to abandon them both.

"Um, this is a cool truck," she finally said, barely holding herself together. "It's um, really big, tall," she couldn't help adding and busted out in laughter so consuming she had to grab her stomach and suddenly had to pee.

Gina joined in her laughter and Vint growled.

"Oh, come on, it's all just a little too on point, don't you think? It had to be said," Gina pointed out.

"I am sure, now do you two want a ride to the cemetery or not?"

"Yes, please," Hailey said between gasps of air. "And the grocery store, we need to get something for dinner."

"Wonderful, shopping with Gina," Vint hissed.

Hailey wasn't sure what that ominous statement would portend but she climbed up into the truck, settling into the middle knowing that she was embracing whatever was happening around her. She was surprised at herself for it, but she hadn't felt this good since her grandmother had gotten sick.

A prickle of guilt entered her at that realization. But she pushed it off because she knew that her happiness wasn't a mark against the love she had for her Grandmother.

"So do all female demons have no horns?" she asked after Vint pulled away from the fence.

"Some do, some don't, it's even more unlikely in half-demon females though. All males—half or not—have horns, and many demons have the red eyes like me. Tails are unlikely in a half-demon, though it happens, and every once in a while, wings! Oh I wish I'd gotten wings like my dad," Gina explained.

"Is he very different than Grail?"

Gina nodded, "They are different species of demon and if you saw them next to each other you'd notice many differences in appendages, overall size, and of course, what they can do with their magic."

The mention of the magic had Hailey's thoughts turning from demon to witch and she looked down at her hands. "Can I do things like you did with the rain and the wine?"

"Everyone's magic is slightly different. You obviously have the same affinity for tea spells like your grandmother because it didn't take much for you to activate one unknowingly, same with your sister, but she also has something in her jewelry work, at least the piece we saw on Summer. Though that could have been a one-off, but I'd guess she could do that sort of thing again if she really cared to."

Hailey nodded and settled into the drive, wondering if there was something else she could do other than tea magic if she wanted. She certainly didn't have an artistic outlet like her sister, so she doubted it.

When they arrived at the cemetery Hailey was about to burst so she peeled off to use the facilities while Vint showed Gina where the grave was.

Vint put his arm around Gina as he led her to the gravesite. "It was a great ceremony, I watched from afar," Vint admitted.

"I tried to be here in time, I just ...I just didn't think she'd actually pass; you know?" Gina's voice broke and black tears slipped out of her eyes.

"I didn't believe it either, when she called me, I thought she was being dramatic, I thought she just wanted us to visit. I hadn't in a while I guess." Vint had beat himself up for it, too. He lived so close and had easy access to Merry, but he had gone more than a month without visiting. The last time he'd been there she'd seemed fine, happy, healthy and telling him that he needed to find a girlfriend. Just like always.

"There was no way to know with her. She never would have told us she was sick, not until she had no options left," Gina said as if reading his mind. "I hadn't seen her in a year, but I talked to her on the phone nearly every week, she never said, not once did she ask me to leave where I was to see her for what might be the last time." Gina's voice was full of hurt and Vint squeezed her tighter.

They got to the grave in the family plot area and squatted to look closer at the beautiful headstone. Gina ran her hand over the name etched there, her whole body shaking with emotion.

"The last time I called, no one answered, I knew then, I could feel it in my gut. It was already too late, and I was so mad at her."

Vint watched his sister fist her hands and he placed his own over them, he understood. It was easier to be angry than sad sometimes.

Gina sniffled and looked at him. "I thought she'd leave it all to you, I didn't think she would break the agreement."

Vint shrugged, he'd been surprised too but his last conversation with Merry had hinted at this very thing. *'When I'm gone, I think you'll all finally find what you need. Take care of my girls, all of them.'*

"Merry wanted us to know each other, you know that she always said she wished it was possible. I think this was her way to force it," Vint said.

"You're not angry? They might decide to keep the magic. We always talked about using it for a safe space."

Vint hugged his sister. "Either way, I'll always take care of you. You know that."

Gina huffed and pushed him away. "I'm perfectly capable of taking care of myself, Vint. I love to travel; the world is great." She gave him a bright smile and stood, brushing the dirt off her knees.

Vint wanted to argue, wanted to point out that she was running, not traveling and she would be better off with a firm place to lay her head, but it was an old argument he knew he'd lose so he didn't say anything.

"You like her, so what's that about?" Gina said, no doubt in an effort to further distract him from the current line of conversation.

"She's annoying, doesn't know what's good for her," Vint snarled.

"You always were a sucker for a damsel in distress."

"She's definitely in distress, but I wouldn't call her a damsel," Vint looked back to where Hailey was currently leaning against his truck, face pointed up toward the sun. Her curvy body showing a lot of skin in her short shorts and t-shirt. Did she realize how tempting she looked right now?

"I think she likes you too," Gina whispered next to him. "She looks at you like she thinks you'd be scary but fun."

"She just lost her grandmother and found out she's a witch, I don't think now's the time to be trying for a roll in the hay, Gina. Not everyone solves their issues with sex."

Gina grinned up at him. "But maybe they should."

Vint didn't respond because he would very much like to solve all of Hailey's problems with time in his bed. The biggest thing stopping him was a feeling that once wouldn't be enough with this little witch, and he'd never experienced the desire for a relationship before.

"Let's go, I don't want to leave Batal alone guarding the house longer than necessary." Vint put his arm around Gina again and they walked back toward Hailey and his truck.

Hailey looked over at them as they approached, a sad smile on her face.

CHAPTER
TEN

Hailey hadn't missed the loving exchange between the siblings, even from a distance she'd seen how Gina shuddered with tears and Vint offered consoling touches. No matter what else these two were, they'd loved her grandmother just as much as she and Kathy did, and they had a sibling bond that was strong. That knowledge made her trust them even more.

"It's a beautiful spot, I know she would love it," Gina said when they got close, her voice still a little rough with tears.

"Thank you, she picked it of course, after her first husband died she bought the whole plot with room to spare. I'm really glad you are here, Gina, I'd love to hear about your time with her." She looked at Vint whose eyes were shaded and hidden. She wanted to know what he was thinking, was he as glad that Hailey and Kathy were around as she was that he and Gina were? "You too, Vint. I would love to know what it was like to be with her when you were young."

Gina smiled brightly. "She took us in when our mother died, we were both young. Vint was twelve and I was eight. She finished raising us and taught us how to use our magics as they showed up. She even cast spells to keep our fathers out so they wouldn't come in and eat their offspring before maturity," Gina shrugged as if it were no big deal. "It's a demon thing."

"How is it that I never knew you two were there with her?"

"We were mostly grown by the time you were born, and although we still called it home base, we both were traveling a lot and trying to make our own way."

"Wait, how old are you?" Hailey gasped then covered her mouth, instantly regretting the rude remark.

Gina laughed. "Demons don't age the same as humans or witches. When you and your sister moved in permanently, we moved out. It was time to leave the nest anyway, no big deal."

"I'm sorry about that." Hailey's guilt swelled despite Gina's statement that it was time, she'd displaced these two.

"No need, like I said, we were grown, you were just kids. You two needed Merry more than we did at that point."

"I suppose my father forbade us from knowing about you two, huh? Was there any overlap there, did you guys live in the house before my father moved out for college?"

"There were a few years, yes. He was a good man," Vint said. "He accepted us as sort of siblings while he was there, and helped us feel comfortable. But he was already focused on living his own life, planning his future. We didn't interact a lot. The block was meant to keep you two safe and happy, innocent of this side of the world. I think it had more to do with your mother's hesitation with anything magical—she was just a human after all."

"Fear can be a very convincing argument," Hailey agreed. It made a lot of *her* decisions.

"It does, and not knowing there are more things to be afraid of isn't a bad thing for children. Innocence can lead to happiness, but it can also put you in danger of being taken advantage of. I saw you and your sister; it was about a month before your parents died and you were staying at your grandmother's house for the weekend. I stopped in to get some tea Merry had made special for me and you two walked right by as if I was anybody else. It was strange because I could smell the witch on you, but you didn't see the demon in me. If I'd wanted to harm you, it would have been too easy."

"That is unnerving. I wonder how many other demons I've walked by in my life and didn't even know it," Hailey said with a little shudder, she didn't like the idea that the world was hiding such important things from her, she had enough anxiety without the addition of demonic beings she couldn't see or recognize.

"Probably a few," Vint said, "But they'd have recognized you no problem and likely tried to hit on you or avoid you."

Hailey gasped, "I might have dated a demon?" she paused, "Actually yeah, that might explain the terrible luck I've had in my love life, except ..."

"What?" Gina prompted.

"I always ran the names of my dates by Grandma, so if it was a demon, she would have told me not to date them, right? I mean a demon wouldn't make a good boyfriend." Hailey bit her lip as she tumbled over the words and watched Vint's eyes darken and his lips thin, he looked like he was barely holding back his anger and she immediately regretted what she'd said. He hadn't been mean or rude, he seemed like a pretty decent guy, if a little magic hungry. He was sexy and definitely her type, aside from the demon thing... which was looking less and less like an issue the more time she spent with him and Gina.

"Oh yeah, I don't date demons. Halfies are okay but I prefer humans," Gina said cheerily.

"That's because they're easier to chew up and spit out," Vint said. "And we both know you've dabbled in shifters, too."

Gina grinned wide, "Oh yeah, shifters are great."

Hailey wondered if Batal's obvious affection for Gina was

because of a past roll in the hay, and not just her stunning looks.

"Honestly there's nothing wrong with dating a demon, but you do have to be careful because their natural inclination is to trick you into some kind of deal or another, and Merry wasn't anti-demon so I doubt she'd have warned you off but there aren't any halfies in Lavender Grove aside from Vint and I."

"Oh, good to know I guess."

"Are we going?" Vint snapped and got in the truck.

"He's a little touchy about the whole anti-demon thing most witches have."

"Oh, I'm not—"

Gina shook her head. "Don't worry, I get it, he's just overly sensitive; he thinks you're hot." She grinned wide and opened the passenger door, cutting off any remark Hailey might have had to respond.

Vint seethed as he drove, frustration boiling beneath the surface. Why did he have to be constantly reminded that someone like her would never want someone like him? Sure, he could likely tempt her into a one night stand she might regret, but she wouldn't look at him and think about flowers, dates, picnics and long lazy mornings in bed. And why. when he looked at her, did he suddenly want those things he'd never wanted in the past.

He needed to keep his head straight, he was here for the magic, he could do a lot of good with it. He needed to concentrate on getting it before it ended up somewhere dangerous like with the coven.

Beside him, Hailey sat quietly, biting at her lower lip and fiddling her fingers nervously. Every time he moved and brushed against her in the tight space of his truck she stiffened, and he was further reminded that she thought he was a horrible beast, a monster.

"Stop fidgeting," he growled.

She dropped her fingers but gripped at the fringe of her shorts, frowning out the window. "Sorry," she whispered.

"What's got your panties in a bunch?" Gina asked him with mirth clear in her voice.

Vint didn't respond because it wasn't *his* panties that were in his thoughts at the moment, and that just pissed him off further.

When they got to the grocery store, they all hopped out of the truck, but Hailey was hesitant.

"I can just run in, if you two want to wait here?" Hailey suggested.

"No way, I love shopping!" Gina said.

Vint looked at Hailey and raised an eyebrow, challenging her to say something about not wanting to be seen shopping with demons.

Thankfully she seemed to decide against it.

"I am thinking chicken and salad for dinner, does that sound alright?" Hailey asked with too much cheer he assumed was masking her anxiety over the situation.

"Fine, maybe some more wine, Gina will drink it all," Vint said.

"Yeah, I can only make the wine fill the glass if the bottle is nearby, can't make wine from air. Oh, and dessert!" Gina added, "something decadent."

Lavender Grove had one large grocery store and so it was always busy. Today was no different and before they'd even gotten halfway through the parking lot Hailey was almost approached twice, but after they spotted who she was with, they gave a curt nod and hurried past instead. Vint didn't care, he had no interest in the coven members' comments, but he hated how it emphasized the position he and Gina were putting Hailey in. Making her an outcast, making enemies of so many in the community.

"Coven members?" Hailey whispered as they entered the store gesturing with her eyes to a couple of young women whispering and glaring in her direction.

Vint grabbed a cart as Gina headed straight for the produce department, head high and a smile on her face. She always acted like she didn't give a shit about what other people thought of her. But Vint knew. He'd comforted her through tears many nights when someone had broken her heart because of what she was, and each time it had killed a part of his respect for the world. "Yep, they know us even if we hide our extra parts," Vint said. "Your grandmother made sure the local witches all met us when she was teaching us, made sure they knew that we were to be accepted in the magical community and not shunned as demons. The younger ones probably only heard rumors of us."

"Oh, that's nice," Hailey said.

"It didn't work," Vint snapped. "That's why they kicked her out of the coven."

"What!" Hailey said, a little too loud as it drew the attention of everyone in the produce section. "What the hell?" she whispered. "I thought maybe Grandma just didn't want to be a part of it, they actually kicked her out and then showed up at her house for her teas and the wake? What the hell?"

Gina grabbed a bag and started filling it with oranges. "Oh yeah, she was outcast until we left, and you and your sister arrived. They tried to get her back then, but she refused. She wanted nothing to do with them after the way they treated us and her."

"So why did they all show up at the house buying teas? If they weren't friends?"

"Some were still friendly with her, behind the coven's back and on the down low," Gina said dramatically. "And of course they all still came to her when they needed tea spells."

"They mostly came to the wake yesterday because they want her magic, they would do anything to keep it from me and Gina," Vint added with a grunt.

Gina put a basket of strawberries into the cart then hurried away to grab blueberries and a bag of grapes.

Vint watched as Gina walked by the price tags and they shifted, going down a dollar here or fifty cents there. Hailey must have noticed too because she blinked and grabbed Vint's arm, leaning close to hiss in his ear. "Did she just—"

The contact made his chest rumble, but he covered it with a laugh. She smiled up at him and let go but not before he heard her inhale. Was she ... smelling him? Deep down in his soul a spark flickered in response and his instincts told him to grab her, to take her to his home and never let her go, hoard this precious woman away from the cruel world.

"We need whipped cream!" Gina shouted and dragged Vint out of his spiraling thoughts.

Vint cleared his throat and stepped slightly away from Hailey, he had to keep himself under control. "Oh yes, the checker will be surprised, but don't worry, the prices go back to normal once she steps out of the store. Anyone who buys before then will get a great deal though."

Hailey cleared her own throat and looked away as if she were having just as hard a time controlling her thoughts and feelings with this closeness. "Lucky me, because I haven't worked in weeks and I'm about to be fired," Hailey said with a laugh.

Vint frowned. He didn't like knowing she might be

struggling. "I can pay for this, like I said, she won't let the total get very high."

Hailey shook her head. "No worries, I am inheriting my grandmother's fortune, remember."

Vint wanted to point out that the time frame for getting the inheritance could be months and there would be things to pay out immediately like taxes and the funeral fees. But he didn't have the right to care, he wasn't Hailey's keeper, her boyfriend, her anything. No matter how much he wanted to tell her that she'd be fine because he would take care of any need she had, now and forever. It wasn't his place and frankly, the impulse made him uncomfortable.

She leaned across him to grab lettuce and he didn't miss the way she inhaled deeply again. His body heated and hardened. Did she want him as much as he wanted her? Could it be possible she was feeling the same draw he was? The thought sent another rumble through his chest.

She froze, lettuce dropping into the cart and her gaze shot to his. His face heated under her scrutiny.

"Salad," he said dumbly.

"Yeah. Let's get the chicken," she said turning quickly and hurrying away from him.

He growled agreement, following her with the cart while Gina continued to flit around and grab anything that struck her fancy, dropping prices as she went. When they were almost done, Gina threw a bag of cat treats into the cart.

"Really, Gina, that's just mean," Vint said.

"What? Batal is my little kitty cat and I like to feed him treats when he's a good boy," she said with a wink.

"You're a horrible person," Vint said, shaking his head because he knew his friend would love anything Gina gave him.

"No, I am a wonderful demon," she corrected.

At the checkout they had an overflowing cart and the price

was so low the poor young checker looked like he was about to call a manager, but Gina leaned forward and pursed her lips and the guy was lost. He took Hailey's card that she insisted on using despite Vint's protests and sent them on their way with a dazed, lovestruck expression. Gina may not have been powerful in the traditional witch sense, but she wielded the allure of sexuality inherited from her sex demon father, and she used it like a magic spell to get people to act the way she wanted.

The price was high though, because when she released a human from the spell, when she wanted true feelings from someone who really knew her, they never accepted what she was. Vint knew how devastating that was for her.

"Where do you think Grail is?" Hailey asked as they loaded the groceries into the back of the truck.

"Bar," Vint and Gina said in unison.

Vint frowned. "He's likely trying to pick up some chick for a quickie before he has to be back at the house."

"A human?" she asked.

"Likely. A witch that's into demons is harder to find. Witches *are* humans though technically, just with an ability to use magic."

"Like a genetic mutation?" Hailey asked with a slight frown.

"I don't think I'd call it a mutation, more like humans are missing something that witches held onto from the beginning of the universe when magic was abundant," Gina said.

"And demons are ..."

"Even older than the beginning of the universe," Vint supplied.

"Is it normal for demons to procreate with humans and witches? *Can* they procreate with humans, or just witches?"

Gina nodded. "Both yes, though a half-demon, half-human is more likely to be trouble. There's something about a witch—a balance in the magic—that helps to suppress some of the more destructive instincts that a demon typically has. Humans don't have a handle on their baser instincts and add a demon in the mix, you end up with a lot of serial killers and psychopaths."

"But, no, it's not normal for a witch to willingly procreate with a demon," Vint said. "Our mother summoned them to her, she was ... a bit of an outcast herself. She dabbled in dark magics and that's what attracted her to demons in the first place. Most witches wouldn't dare sully themselves with demons or their magic," Vint's voice turned a bit bitter even as he tried to keep himself even. He grabbed the now empty cart and turned to take it back across the lot.

Gina jumped onto the front of the cart demanding a ride and they left Hailey to herself by the truck.

"You know you glare at her a lot," Gina said.

"So? I'm not trying to be her friend; I'm trying to keep her from letting the magic go to the coven."

"Maybe you *should* try to be her friend," Gina pointed out. "Sometimes friends become lovers, brother. Some of the best kind, actually, because when you're already friends, you already know each other's secrets."

CHAPTER
ELEVEN

Hailey watched the two walk away and wanted to kick herself. She just couldn't stop herself from accidentally offending the man. And she felt a pang of regret every time, wanted to reach out and touch him, tell him she was sorry, she didn't see him as a terrible scary demon. She also longed to bury her face in his neck and memorize his scent. She'd been enjoying it in the truck and missed it as soon as she was out. But when she caught it again in the grocery store she hadn't been able to stop herself from inhaling as much as possible. He was sweet, spicy and musky, and she wanted to lick it up.

An older gentleman she recognized as her third-grade teacher, Mr. Pentack, hurried across the lot to her. "Hailey Silver what the hell do you think you're doing?"

"Excuse me?" Had he read her lascivious thoughts from across the parking lot? Did he know she was lusting after a half-demon? Did he know about demons and witches? *Shit, was her third-grade teacher a witch?*

"I know what they are, you are messing with some serious trouble young lady. You need to let the coven handle this."

Hailey narrowed her eyes at the man. He was just like the

other coven members. Bigots, that's what they were, elitist bigots, and she wanted nothing to do with them. She was glad her grandmother had found herself on the outs with the coven because they were not good people.

"You know what, Mr. Pentack, I think I will do whatever the hell I want, demons and all," she whispered, leaning close and meeting his eyes. "My grandmother didn't want anything to do with the coven and neither do I. Her magic won't be used to discriminate."

His eyes widened and he stepped back. "You'll regret this, girl," he snapped and practically ran away as Vint and Gina strode back toward her. Vint tracked the retreating man with a glower and looked like he'd prefer chasing him down and letting him know what a demon could really do.

Not that Hailey knew what that was, but she had a pretty good idea. She couldn't help feeling comforted by Vint's obvious protectiveness. She'd never had a man look so willing to do violence on her behalf before.

Though she had to remind herself that it was also self-serving, Vint needed her to relinquish the magic to him, so he didn't want anyone to give her any other ideas.

"Who was that lovely gentleman?" Gina asked with a frown.

"Witch, probably a coven member. Fuck, they are everywhere, how did my grandmother handle it?"

"She was strong, they knew better than to approach her, she could magic them into dust, and besides, they all relied on her and her spells. You know she sold to them constantly, even as they bad mouthed her and pooh-poohed her lifestyle. They took from her," Vint snarled.

"Merry just wanted to help people, even those who wouldn't have helped her," Gina said.

"She was too good for them," Hailey said.

"She was," they both agreed.

The drive to the house was a bit more somber, each of them lost to their own thoughts.

As soon as they pulled up to her grandmother's house Hailey had a feeling that something wasn't right. Vint and Gina got out of the truck and stared across the yard, obviously feeling the same way.

"What is it?" Hailey asked, moving instinctively closer to Vint. It may be for selfish reasons, but she knew he'd protect her.

"I'm not sure, but I hope Batal is okay," Vint said darkly then strode forward.

"He has nine lives, he's fine," Gina said but there was a higher pitch to her voice that told Hailey, Gina cared for the cat man even if she didn't want to admit it.

They left the groceries in the truck and walked slowly toward the house. There was an eerie feeling as they passed the magic-eaten portion of the gardens, everything withered and grey. Hailey could sense the absence of life and magic there and it made her shiver. She'd been too distracted earlier when they'd passed to give it much thought, but it added to the uneasy feeling in her stomach now. As soon as they crossed the line where Vint had stopped the magic-eaters it was like stepping into a warm hug, the scents and feelings of life and what she now recognized as her grandmother's magic enveloped her and she sighed with relief.

"Do humans feel that?" she wondered aloud.

"No, they might get a little chill oddly at times or goosebumps for no reason sort of thing, you likely did as well, while you were bound. It's usually a magic-related response but they don't recognize it as such. It takes a large concentration of magic to even make a human react that much though," Gina explained.

When they got to the base of the steps they paused and looked up at the house, there was a sheen around it, like a slight distortion in the air stretching the length of the front of the house.

"What is that?" Hailey asked.

"That is a protection spell," Vint said and reached out a hand. He hissed and pulled back, "keeping us out."

"What!" Hailey gasped and stepped forward, reaching out she felt a tingle but no pain, she stepped through the spell and onto the steps, turning to face Vint and Gina who looked at her with worried expressions.

Vint lifted his hand as if he wanted to grab her and pull her back, but the invisible barrier stopped him. "You should come back over here; we'll figure this out but it's not safe to be separated."

"Batal!" Gina yelled.

Hailey shook her head, trying for a confidence she didn't actually feel. Her stomach was twisted into nervous knots and her palms were sweaty. "This is my house, my grandmother's house, I am going in there and seeing who the fuck thinks they can just take over." She was angry, someone was trying to steal from them. She turned and went up the steps.

"Dammit, Hailey, just wait!" Vint called but she didn't stop.

She strode to the front door.

"Call your dad." Hailey heard Gina snap at Vint.

Hailey opened the front door and walked in. The door slammed behind her, and she held her breath for a moment, waiting to be attacked.

"Hailey, dear, come, come join us."

Hailey followed the voice into the living room and found a gathering of witches—they had to be. Seven of them all looking at her expectantly. She recognized them and not just from the wake, but they'd all come to her grandmother time and again, buying tea, having a quick chat and leaving with a smile. Among them were the two nosy neighbors Mrs. Hilltop and Mrs. Jenson, both looking smug. The one who'd spoken was the youngest of the group, Beatrix Pulcifer, the owner of a little café downtown. She'd moved to Lavender Grove just last year, she had mocha dark skin and black curls, she was beautiful and friendly, and Hailey had spoken with her many times, but never would she have foreseen this situation. Suddenly, it made sense why her grandmother had always declined to meet her at the café for lunch.

"Beatrix, what is the point of this little takeover? You can't really think this is how things are best resolved." Hailey said, keeping her tone calm and firm.

"We tried to be reasonable, but time is short and it seems you aren't coming around to our way of thinking. And you have accepted those demons into your home," Beatrix said with a shudder. "You know I doubted the rumors when I first arrived, I thought there was no way there were two young witches here who had no idea what they were, but it's true, isn't it?" Beatrix's face took on a sad and placating softness. "You had no idea you were a witch, and you didn't know how dangerously your grandmother was living her life. I am here to help now, you don't know what you are dealing with out there, what they are is evil, no matter the pretty and tempting package."

Hailey couldn't deny some of that, but she also knew that her grandmother had always made decisions that were well thought out and fair and what her grandmother wanted after she died was to keep her magic away from the people she didn't trust to do good with it.

When Hailey didn't respond Mrs. Hilltop chimed in. "We are here to take over the magic. We know it's such a huge drain for someone like you to try and handle, someone untrained and caught unaware, so unfair of your grandmother to keep you in the dark all these years. We just want to help. Can you show us where your grandmother kept her recipe book?" Mrs. Hilltop asked sweetly.

Panic gripped Hailey and her gaze swept over the bookshelves in the room. They looked fine but something was off. She couldn't put her finger on it, but she knew these nosey witches had rummaged around her grandmother's things and it pissed her off. Hailey snapped her gaze back to the eager faces and crossed her arms over her chest. "No."

"No?" Mrs. Hilltop gasped. "What do you mean, *no*, girl? You are in way over your head!"

Beatrix reached out and laid a hand on Mrs. Hilltop's arm, stopping her from continuing her rant. "We understand that this is a stressful time, and I know how your anxiety controls so much of your life," she said in a calm tone as if approaching a wild animal. "You don't need to be overwhelmed, Hailey, we are here to help."

Hailey gritted her teeth. How dare this woman use that against her, those offhand comments she'd made in the café in passing, about why she didn't drive, why she needed decaf most days. "I am not now, nor will I ever be handing over anything of my grandmother's to you ungrateful witches. You abandoned her because she was willing to help a couple of children. But you weren't above using her for her gifts, were you? Constantly stopping by at all hours for her tea to help with whatever you weren't powerful enough to fix yourself." Hailey let her disdain show on her face.

Mrs. Hilltop's face softened. "Is that what they told you? You can't trust demons, even half-witch ones. They are not being honest with you. Think about it. We have all been friends with your grandmother for years. We all came to her for teas, yes, she helped us because we are friends. Do you really think we'd have kept doing that if we'd shunned her?"

Hailey knew the woman's words were reasonable but there was something there that she didn't trust, a feeling that was wrong and she definitely didn't get that same wrong feeling when Vint and Gina spoke of the situation. She trusted her gut, just like her grandmother taught her. *Hailey, your gut tells you things your eyes can't see, your ears can't hear, and your mind can't comprehend. If your gut tells you not to drive a car, don't. If it tells you the man asking for a date is a snake, he is! There is more to this world than you will know for most of your life, but never forget that if you continue to trust your instincts, your gut, you cannot make the wrong choice.*

And now her gut told her there were seven snakes in front of her, power hungry and willing to do anything to get what they wanted. But she also knew that she had to tread carefully, she was alone with them and there was a powerful force keeping out the ones she thought she *could* trust. "I haven't made a decision yet, it's mine and my sister's to make and we won't be pressured, not by you, not by demons. No one," she stated firmly. "I want you all to leave and let us make our decision in our own time, respect our grief, respect our grandmother's wishes."

Mrs. Hilltop's face turned red, and a man stood, putting his hand on her back. James Connery, a gardener who had come to her grandmother for advice more than once with how to improve his and his clients' gardens. He was just a bit older than Hailey, he'd been in school with Kathy and had always seemed like a decent guy, of course her grandmother had never invited him in for tea when he stopped for advice, so that spoke to how she felt about the man.

"Stop. We can't force her, not like this." He turned blue eyes to Hailey. "Will you at least hear us out, let us make our case?"

Hadn't they already, she wondered. What more could they say? "Where's Batal? He should still be in here, if you've harmed him, I won't be caring about anything coming out of your mouths."

"He chased a mouse outside and that's when we enacted the spell to keep everyone but you and your sister out," James explained.

"Release the spell," Hailey demanded.

"And let those demons back in?" an older woman, retired real estate agent Betty Whitford, gasped.

"Right now I trust them more than you all," Hailey pointed out. "They have made no demands of me, only helped me to understand what's going on."

Beatrix snapped her fingers and seconds later the front door flew open. Vint was the first one in quickly followed by Gina, Grail, and Batal.

Hailey held up a hand to stop them from whatever they might have been about to do as they snarled coming into the room. Vint and Batal flanked her, clearly showing their intention to protect. Hailey couldn't help smiling as a warm feeling embraced her. The coven wanted her to think she was alone and vulnerable, overwhelmed and about to be taken advantage of by demons. But they were so wrong, she'd never felt so protected, empowered and strong in her own self. These demons and cat shifter, were strengthening her, not trying to break her down for their advantage.

"That was a cheap trick," Batal hissed. "Sending in a mouse."

"Hailey, are you alright?" Vint asked, his eyes narrowed on the witches.

"I'm fine, they were rude and underhanded, but they haven't harmed me."

"Yet," Vint growled.

"Now talk. Make your case," Hailey demanded of the coven.

Beatrix was the one to speak, apparently their leader. "We know how to use the magic; we know how to properly and safely cast a spell. Those recipes of your grandmother's could be dangerous in the wrong hands. Even in the hands of an inexperienced witch like yourself they could cause trouble. Did you know that yours was the only house that got rained on this afternoon? I heard people talking of it, such a strange occurrence," Beatrix said smugly.

Hailey stiffened slightly because that was definitely true. She'd already proven that by accidentally summoning Grail too. Not that she'd ever admit it to these witches. She and Kathy were inexperienced, but these witches wanted to take everything, they didn't want to teach them how to handle it. They weren't looking for a way to honor her grandmother.

As if reading her mind, James spoke. "We just want to make sure that your grandmother's legacy goes on in her spell work and that her magic finds a safe place to settle."

"I understand," Hailey said, and the coven's faces filled with hope. Beside her Vint stiffened. "But I am not going against my grandmother's wishes, and she was adamant that if my sister and I don't want the magic, it goes to Vint. Those were her wishes and I see no reason to deny them."

"That bitch!" Across the room Penny Trible burst out aggressively and the others scowled at Hailey.

Hailey glared back. "Now, I suggest you all leave and do not come back."

"Hailey—" Mrs. Hilltop started but Beatrix touched her arm and she stopped.

"We are not a violent coven," Beatrix said. "We understand that your grandmother chose to go a way we couldn't accept. Just think about it, okay, remember that a demon is tricky, and they may have fooled your grandmother, but you don't have to let them fool you too. And Hailey," Her voice turned silky smooth and her face softened into a worried smile. "Make sure you aren't making decisions based on your anxiety-ridden mind."

"Bitch," Gina snarled and bared her teeth at the girl. Batal put an arm around Gina and Hailey hoped that would keep the demon from lashing out. The last thing they needed was to give the coven more reason to hate anyone with demon blood.

With those parting words, the coven filed out, each one turning their noses up as they passed, as if being so close to demons was a disgusting thing to be forced upon them. But Gina, Vint and Grail stood their ground and when the door shut behind the last coven witch, Hailey ran to the kitchen.

TWELVE

"Where's the book? And get all the leftover funeral food out of here. I don't trust anything they make," Hailey ordered.

"Already on it," Vint said opening the fridge and grabbing armfuls of half-eaten casseroles. He stalked outside then Hailey heard an explosion and saw a small burst of light out the kitchen window.

"That's one way to do it," she said with a laugh. "But where the hell is the book?"

"I put it here," Batal said opening the oven. "As soon as you all left, I had a bad feeling, it's a lot of responsibility to watch this place. So I figured I would hide that at least and hope for the best."

Hailey grabbed the book and clutched it to her chest. "Anything they want is something worth hiding," she agreed. "Do you think they'll be back?"

Vint nodded. "Until you and Kathy make a decision, the magic is unsettled and sort of bouncing around here looking for where to land. They can feel that. It's vulnerable and if they were powerful enough, they *could* just take it from you."

Hailey frowned, knowing that he was chastising her.

"The coven isn't that powerful, and the magic isn't that desperate yet," Grail snarled at his son. "So maybe you quit acting like she needs to rush into things."

Vint bared his teeth back at his father and Hailey put herself between the two, amazed by the fact that she felt perfectly safe standing between two snarling demons.

"They can't just take it, that's good, the magic is going to go where we tell it to, and it will just have to chill until Kathy and I figure out where that is going to be."

"Magic isn't always predictable," Vint pointed out. "And at times has a mind of its own. It could get tired of waiting for you to make a choice, or it could be tempted away by someone it finds interesting, powerful or not."

"You're not that interesting," Grail mumbled, and Hailey heard Gina giggle. Vint glared.

Hailey shook her head. "You're talking about it like it's a person."

Vint nodded. "It sort of is. Most witch families see their magic as another family member. They will talk to it and they will try to please it. If they have darker tendencies, their magic will turn dark and start craving sacrifices."

"What!"

"Don't worry, the Honeycomb magic was never like that. It simply wants to be used, so think about that too. If you don't plan to use it, it isn't wise to keep it. Magic can get bored and then it may start to cause trouble all on its own."

"What kind of trouble?"

"Little things at first, like hiding your car keys or rearranging furniture, typical poltergeist sort of things except it isn't a ghost, it's the magic."

"Okay, something to consider, I guess." And talk to her sister about. "For now I want this book somewhere where no one is going to find it. I'm not sure in this house is that place."

Hailey hated the idea of being separated from the book. She felt a pull in her belly telling her that it was a necessary item, like her wallet or cellphone. She was tempted to soothe it and tell it that she was only thinking of temporarily hiding it away but then she stopped herself. It was a book; it didn't have feelings ... right?

Hailey gave the book a little loving pat just in case.

"I know where you can hide it that the coven would never consider going, follow me," Vint said. "You three unload the groceries, search the house for spells, and if Kathy and Summer show up, fill them in."

Hailey followed Vint, still clutching the book, not sure where he was going to take her. He headed outside and she assumed they'd go to his truck, but he went in the direction of the wooded area that ran along the right side of her grandmother's property. He looked at her with a flicker of nervousness crossing his features a couple times, but she just smiled and kept pace, trusting him. Nothing in her gut was telling her to hesitate and she even had the odd feeling that the book was calm, understanding that this was for the best and only temporary.

Vint stopped when they'd walked far enough into the trees that they couldn't see the house any longer. It smelled like pine and sap mixed with a wetness that reminded her of dark earth and moss. It was pleasant, smelled like life. Vint lifted a hand and the air around them shifted. In front of him an oval swirling of black and red opened to a hole.

"My home," Vint said, holding a hand out to her. "Come on, it won't harm you," he said with a smile. "Trust me?"

"I do, but what is this?" she asked, taking a hesitant step forward.

"It's a portal, Merry helped me make it so that I could always be close no matter what. She could call me for help or anything any time," he said, clearing his throat as if the reminder that Merry was gone had put a lump there.

Hailey took his hand, squeezing in sympathy. She didn't know how long his grief would last, but she recognized it as strongly in him as she felt in herself. Merry had been a mother to him and Gina when they needed it, just like she'd been to Hailey and Kathy. And that kind of care and dedication made a lasting impression.

"I'm excited to see how a half-demon, half-witch lives," she said with a grin.

His eyes flashed with something she couldn't name and then, hand in hand they stepped through the swirl of air. Hailey felt a little tingle of magic as she emerged on the other side. She had expected to fall, to whoosh and spin, maybe feel a little motion sick, but aside from the tingle, it had felt like stepping forward, nothing more.

She immediately turned and was looking at the same swirl, but on the other side was the forest they'd just left. It closed before her eyes and disappeared, leaving her wherever the hell she was. A moment of anxiety threatened to take hold of her mind, but she breathed in the scent she'd come to know as Vint and it immediately soothed her worry.

She bit her lip and twirled around slowly, hoping he hadn't caught her almost panic, taking the place in. The room they stood in was spacious with bookshelves along two walls and comfortable furniture she could imagine curling up on with a book and not wanting to move for hours. She itched to go to the shelves and read the titles, what kind of books did a half-demon, half-witch like to read? She wanted to know but she didn't want to invade his privacy. She had a feeling this wasn't something he did often, not judging by the anxious way he watched her, almost as if he wanted to change his mind and shoo her back out immediately. There were no windows she noticed, the only light was coming from a few flickering bulbs overhead and one lamp in the corner. Were they still in Lavender Grove? The U.S.? Earth? She had no clue, and it should have made her more anxious than excited, but it didn't.

"Where exactly are we?"

"The demon realm," he said as if it was no big deal.

"The demon realm!" she gasped. "Like where I summoned Grail up from?"

Vint nodded. "It's another dimension, not even exactly on earth, but sort of beside it, coexisting but not touching. It's hard to explain."

"So you can't get here without a portal or a summoning? I couldn't dig a hole and find your backyard?" she teased.

"No, thankfully, otherwise it would be hellacious trying to keep the fangirls away," he teased back, his lips lifting in a smile.

Hailey's stomach did a little flip, was it from the smile or was it the thought of unsuspecting human girls fawning over him, not even seeing the real him but thinking he was the hottest thing they'd ever seen. She cleared her throat and looked away from his darkening eyes. "Are there a lot of portals then, so that you guys can travel back and forth?"

"You can't make a portal without a demon *and* a witch, so it doesn't happen often. And it has to be recharged every once in a while, so some that were made in the past have fizzled out. It's for the best, you wouldn't want demons to have free reign up there."

"So why would a witch make a portal with a demon if they are so dangerous?"

Vint gave her a meaningful look and lifted an eyebrow. His gaze swept down her body slowly and back up.

Heat exploded in Hailey and his meaning was unmistakable. A witch would make a portal for a demon to come to her in her bedroom, because, like Vint and Gina's mom, she might find one irresistible. She wondered what that would be like, all fire and passion she imagined, and how much like a demon lover was Vint?

Hailey looked away to stop her thoughts there, the look of heat in Vint's eyes made her feel like he was reading her mind. "This is where Grail lives then too, where I brought him from when I summoned him?" she asked, her voice husky.

She thought she heard Vint take a sharp breath behind her, but she wasn't sure.

"Yeah, most demons can't go over for any extended period of time. I can because of my half-witch blood. Full demons can live above while fulfilling a summons or for no more than twelve hours before they start to fade."

"Fade?"

"Die," he said with a casual shrug, "They need the magic of the demon realm to sustain themselves, if they aren't supplemented by the magic of a witch and her summoning. While a demon is under a summons he can use the witch as a sort of battery, drawing her energy to stave off earthside death."

Hailey wasn't sure how she felt about being Grail's battery, so she moved on from that quickly. "And a half-demon, half-human, they do fine living above?"

He grunted agreement.

"You don't think highly of other half-human demons, do you?" Hailey asked curiously.

"In my experience they are a nasty species, always trying to be more demon than witch and they think the way to do that is to hurt others and be a general asshole. I think a lot of that attitude though comes from their upbringing, they don't have a safe place to belong, no one accepts them and it's easier to try and be more of an asshole demon than more of a decent witch."

"Hm, maybe I've dated a few of those," she said with a sardonic laugh.

"You should never be mistreated, Hailey."

Hailey turned around and found he'd moved closer while she had been avoiding his dark and knowing gaze. He reached up and pushed a lock of her hair behind her ear.

"You are pure sweet sunshine, just like your grandmother always described."

"I'm a mess," she said, her voice shaky. She wanted to lean forward, wanted to kiss his red lips, to know what a demon might do with his tongue.

"No, you are a witch whose magic has been straining to get out for years, it would make anyone anxious."

She wanted to believe that, wanted so badly to not be a complete mess, but it didn't change the fact that her life was in shambles, getting worse by the day and the only hope of putting it in some semblance of right would be to dismantle everything her grandmother had created in her long life. Sell it all and take the money. She looked down at the book, the reason they had come down here. She needed to focus, just like the counselor at school used to tell her, one thing at a time. "So we can keep the book here? What about other demons, will they try to take it?"

Vint looked disappointed by the change of subject, but he stepped back and nodded. "It's safe, it wouldn't do them any good anyway. Demons can't work witch magic."

Hailey was comforted by that statement but uncertainty lingered as she handed him the book. He walked to the bookshelf and stuck it between a couple others where it blended in as if it belonged. No one would ever suspect what it was. She gazed closely at the books and noticed that the spines for many of them were in languages she didn't recognize or couldn't read, the few in English seemed to be fairy tales and almanacs their titles hinting at secrets waiting to be uncovered.

"What an interesting collection," she said, reaching out to touch one that caught her eye. It was red leather and the unidentifiable writing on the spine was gold. It shimmered in the low light of the room beckoning her touch. When her finger connected with it she pulled back with a hiss.

"Don't touch," he warned too late, "those demon books tend not to allow anyone other than their owner to touch them."

"Thanks for the warning," she griped and stuck her finger in her mouth. "Anything else here going to try and kill me?"

He grimaced. "No, just the books."

"Seems like a good deterrent from anyone trying to come find the recipe book then, thanks for letting me bring it here." Hailey looked at Vint. His hood had slipped back, and his dark eyes were intent on her again, sending another tingle through her body. She felt like she could get lost in those dark eyes, swallowed up whole and all with a smile on her face.

"You're welcome," he said and grabbed her hand. Never breaking eye contact, he brought her still burning finger close to his face. He pursed his lips and blew on it gently. The soft touch of his breath replaced the burning immediately and the pain eased to a dull pulse.

"Cool trick," she whispered, a little breathless at the closeness of him. The touch of his hand on hers was warm and his lips curved up into a smile showing perfect white teeth.

"I have better tricks," he said with a wink that made the simple statement feel naughty.

She pulled her hand away and cleared her throat because she was far too tempted to ask *like what?* "Can I see the rest of your place?" she asked impulsively instead, not wanting this little trip out of Lavender Grove to end just yet. She figured it would be good to know everything she could about this guy before she made any decisions about whether or not to give him the magic.

He looked surprised by her request but then smiled and swept his hand around the room. "This is my library and living room. Bathroom there," he pointed to a door. "Follow me this way," he said and walked toward the only other door in the place.

THIRTEEN

Vint's body was lighting up with feelings he knew he shouldn't be having. Not for her, one of Merry's precious granddaughters. He ached to pull her to him, his mouth watering as he thought about sticking the finger she'd just put in her mouth straight into his own. He wanted to taste her, to devour her. Most terrifyingly, to keep her.

He'd never brought a woman like her into his space before and he wondered if that was messing with his instincts somehow. He'd brought Gina and Merry of course, but it never felt anything like this, they'd felt like an intrusion in his space, an annoyance at best, not the perfect last addition. It was rattling him, and his body was reacting as if she were his, why else would she be in his space if she wasn't, right? A dark part of his mind reasoned that he could keep her here, there was no escape if he didn't allow it, she could be his forever.

He pushed that dangerous voice away and walked toward the kitchen with a stiffening body. He quickly moved so the island in the center was between them, willing his body's reactions to calm down as she looked around with interest. He wondered what she thought of the place. This room was the most modern in his house. Clean lines, black appliances, and grey countertops. Utilitarian but also sleekly welcoming.

"Do you do a lot of cooking?" she asked.

"Yes, for myself," he added then wished he hadn't, wondering if it had made him sound pathetic. As if he had no friends or lovers.

"I always had trouble cooking for one. I usually eat instant stuff, quick and easy or delivery," she said with a shrug.

Why did it make him so happy to know that she wasn't entertaining other males on a regular basis?

"No delivery in the demon realm," he said with a grunt and then headed to the hallway. "Bedroom this way."

His bedroom was decorated with dark furniture and rich red and black fabrics. His large bed dominated the space, although it was only him who'd ever been in it, choosing to take any of his one-night stands in the woman's bed or a cheap hotel. It was just easier than explaining the whole demon thing to a half-drunk human. He had wanted comfort for himself where he nested though. Lots of pillows and soft blankets and he wondered what Hailey thought of it. Did it appeal to her, or did she see it as messy? He didn't want to care but he did, he held his breath as he stood back and watched her walk in, looking at his things with interest. She ran a finger over the bedspread, and he wondered if that spot would smell like her now. He half wanted to drop down and push his face into it to see. But that would be ridiculous, she'd surely think him insane.

What the hell was wrong with him, why was he suddenly feeling so uncontrolled? He shook himself and concentrated on her, she peeked into the attached bathroom and walk in closet.

"Wow, I'm jealous, that closet is amazing."

"Thanks," he said shortly, making her look at him with pink tinged cheeks. Shit, he'd embarrassed her. He wanted to apologize, to explain that his body was defying him, that his mind was scrambling, and he wasn't sure what the hell was going on but it was taking everything he had not to grab her and throw her down on that bed and maybe never let her back up again.

"We should probably head back," she said, twisting her hands in front of her. "I'm sure my sister will be there by now. Thanks for letting me snoop in your space."

He nodded and walked back to the library knowing she followed, he could feel her, like a tangible link to his groin.

"No windows ... and no door to outside," she commented as they went.

"No. The demon realm isn't very scenic, or safe for someone like me," he admitted. "I only portal in and out of the house and trust me, there's nothing worth seeing through a window."

"So you live in a box down here?"

He turned and saw a look of pity on her face that made him angry. That was not a look he ever wanted to see her direct at him. "Yeah," he snapped. "I also go up top and roam as I wish." That wasn't really true, he had to hide from witches up there and any human he interacted with didn't see the real him.

Her expression turned contemplative. "What would gaining my grandmother's magic do for you?"

He was caught off guard by the question and answered honestly. "If I had a full witch's magic I would be able to glamour myself well enough to trick even witches into not noticing what I am. I wouldn't have to worry about them trying to kill me for going to a restaurant or bar."

"Oh," she said, guilt filling her face now.

That look was just as bad as the pity but for a different reason. He hated to think he'd caused her to feel that way. This wasn't her fault; this wasn't her doing or choice. His mother had made the dumb decision to have a child with a demon, the witches had made the uninformed decision to discriminate against him. This whole situation with the magic now was Merry's doing, and although he wasn't happy about it, he had to respect that these were Merry's last wishes they were all dealing with.

Merry had cared for him but her first duty was to her genetic family and the girls were her first choice to receive the magic he was so desperate for. It would change their lives too, and he didn't think they even really comprehended how much.

When they arrived back at the house the groceries were put away, Summer and Kathy had returned, and everyone was sipping tea. Grail gave him a raised eyebrow look full of meaning, drifting his eyes from Vint to Hailey.

"You two were gone a while," Grail drawled as he leaned against the kitchen counter eating a bag of chips.

Vint met his father's gaze and glared. He knew what the demon was trying to imply, and he didn't like that Grail thought Vint would take advantage of Hailey while she was grieving, or that Hailey would be the type of girl to jump into bed with a near stranger.

"Where the hell did you two go?" Kathy demanded.

"Did they tell you what happened with the coven?" Hailey asked her sister as they embraced.

"Yeah, where did you hide the book?"

Hailey looked at Vint who just shrugged, it didn't matter if everyone knew where the book was, no one could get in.

"Vint's place," Hailey said.

"Oh." Kathy's face was full of surprise. "He lives in Lavender Grove?"

"Yeah, sort of," Hailey said and bit her lip. "He has a portal to the demon realm."

Summer and Kathy both nodded and hummed, taking in

the information better than Vint would have expected. Hailey looked like she was expecting her sister to start freaking out and it irritated Vint. Why the hell was Hailey so worried about what Kathy thought. The woman was her sister, not her keeper.

"Is it nice there?" Summer asked Vint, real curiosity on her face that surprised him.

"No," Vint laughed, "At least not for a half-demon, demons can be quite the purists," he grumbled and sent a glare to Grail who was dumping the remnants of the chips into his wide open mouth.

"Is the demon realm hard for you to live in?" Hailey asked Grail.

He shook his head, chip crumbs flying off his face. "No, I am powerful and feared there, it's great! Though I do so enjoy my stints up here with the humans. There's just something about a soft human or witch body," he ran his hands through the air as if shaping a womanly form and grunted. "Not to mention the better food and drink." He wadded up the chip bag and tossed it to the trash.

"Of course," Vint said with an eye roll, Grail was predictable, all about the selfish pleasures of the flesh and power he could gain through fear. Vint was lucky to have been raised by a caring witch, even if she did have a bit of a demon fetish. "The sun will be going down soon, we need to set up a perimeter to keep the magic-eaters out," Vint said, changing the subject. "Grail, why don't you be useful and help me outside."

Grail nodded and stood, following Vint out to the front yard. As soon as they reached the line in the garden where the magic-eaters had stopped the night before, Vint spun and faced his father.

"What was that look about when we arrived back here, you know I'm not like you. I don't take advantage of whoever I can, and Hailey is definitely not that type of girl."

Grail laughed and poked a finger at his son. "You felt it, didn't you? I wondered. You've been watching that woman like she was something special you couldn't figure out. You felt it when she was in your place, didn't you?"

"What are you talking about?" Vint snapped, wanting to deny he'd felt anything but at the same time, desperate to know why he'd felt like he needed to lock her away and keep her forever while she was in his home. He'd never wished for fatherly advice in his life but now he was hanging on Grail's next words like a lifeline.

"It's a demon thing," Grail shrugged. "When a woman is in a demon's personal space like that, there is a desperation, a need, an overwhelming instinct to keep her, hoard her, and devour her." Grail's eyes turned red and burned from an internal fire as he spoke.

"I didn't want to hurt her," Vint whispered, his voice rough and unsure.

"No, a demon doesn't mean to harm the one they love and keep. But you would inadvertently. You would keep her away from everything she knows and loves, away from the sun and fresh air. You would consume her every thought and moment and eventually she would just ..." Grail flitted his fingers.

Vint shook his head. "That's not what I wanted," he insisted.

"Isn't it? Mind my warning, boy. That woman in there deserves better than a demon mate. If you think you care for her, stay away." He shrugged. "That's why I stick with one-night rolls, your mother was the closest I ever came to a real relationship and that only lasted until I knocked her up."

"Then she broke it off and closed the portal so you wouldn't come after me," Vint said, he knew the story well. Vint looked at the house and saw the shadow of Hailey move across the window. The memory of her hand in his as he'd healed her finger, the smell of her body so close to his, and the sight of her in his bedroom.

He wasn't sure he *could* stay away.

"Get the magic and move on," Grail whispered. "It's for the best, Merry wouldn't have wanted you to destroy her granddaughter."

No, she definitely wouldn't have wanted that. Merry should have known better than to throw them into this situation actually. Anger filled Vint, this was unfair and cruel, this was bullshit. He embraced the anger because it was a safer feeling than the desperation and depression that had filled him at his father's grim warning.

"Merry should have done better," he snapped.

Grail's eyes glinted mischievously at Vint.

Vint's gut soured at the knowledge that he'd said something his father approved of. "Help me set a wall, I don't want to come talk to the magic-eaters tonight."

Together the two men managed to set up a strong barrier that would repel the magic-eaters, mostly by distorting the flow of magic from the garden and house. Magic-eaters were mindless things, floating around at night looking for bits and pieces of unguarded magic easy to consume. This should be enough to trick them, and they'd pass right by.

"Thanks," Vint said as they headed back inside.

"Part of the deal, I have to protect the one who brought me over."

Vint paused and looked back at the still growing portion of garden. "There's a lot here that needs to be gathered before it's no good," he commented.

"Witch's work," Grail said dismissively.

Yelling from inside the house stopped Vint from responding to his father's rude comment. Both men ran for the house and into the living room where Hailey and Kathy were facing off across the room.

"Why the hell didn't you tell me you were going to be fired? How could you let this happen again. Hailey, you have to grow up, you have to take some fucking responsibility for your life," Kathy yelled.

"I am an adult, Kathy. I can make my own damn decisions and that job is not my life. I don't even care about it. They are assholes, obviously, for firing me while I'm grieving so why would I want to work there anyway?"

"Because you have no money, Hailey, none. I know—I was at your apartment today. I got your mail for you; you're welcome. The bills are piled up unpaid and your landlady stopped me to say that you're late with the rent. thank god *she* is being understanding about the situation." Kathy paused and took a deep breath, looking resigned. "Summer and I can't bail you out, Hailey. We are saving up for our wedding. I can't keep taking care of you." The last was a strangled shout and Kathy's face fell in sorrow. "I have my own life to live. Summer and I want our own children and we can't afford to take care of you too."

"Fuck you," Hailey whispered, tears streaming down her face. "I never asked you to help me, you just invaded my privacy *again*, assuming I can't take care of myself and now you're mad because you think you have to do these things, but I never asked, Kathy. I will be fine, I *am* fine."

Vint looked from one sister to the other, trying to process everything being said. He ached to go to Hailey and wrap her in his arms, protect her from her sister's upsetting words, but he had no right and he doubted she'd welcome him anyway.

"How, how will you be fine? No job and almost no place to live."

Hailey lifted her chin in defiance. "I'll live here. And I'll find work."

Kathy stiffened. "Oh no, we agreed, this house sells," she said firmly.

"So you and Summer can have your dream wedding and a fancy honeymoon?" Hailey accused.

"That's not fair," Kathy whispered. "You know that's not fair. I would trade anything to have Grandma back, but it doesn't work that way. Now I am trying to make the best of it. You know this place is expensive to upkeep. We agreed, it's too much for either of us to take on and we could *both* use the cash."

Hailey shook her head, "That was before."

"Before what?" Kathy groaned, throwing up her hands in frustration.

Hailey looked at Vint and Grail as if it were obvious. "Before we knew everything, do you really want to just give up Grandma's magic, what if it's the only thing that makes you able to design such amazing jewelry? Did you ever consider that? What if we give it all up and you lose your talent?"

Kathy touched a silver charm at her neck. "I highly doubt my talent is related to her magic."

"It could be," Grail offered in a bored tone. "You are both magically inclined, even if you were bound from it. The magic would have leaked into you anyway and if you choose to let the family magic go, you could lose even that bit."

Vint watched the whole thing with mixed emotions. He wanted the magic for himself, but he could see how desperate Hailey was to keep what little she had left of her grandmother. It twisted his heart to think of her being forced to let it go just because her sister wanted money, such a stupid reason to give up something as amazing as they could have here. Of course they didn't really know what they could have here, and he'd been trying to keep that from them, to swing them to his side.

He didn't know what to hope for now, so he said nothing.

"We wouldn't be able to see demons for what they are? Or the ghosts?" Hailey asked Grail.

"Maybe not, it's easily hidden from simple human eyes," Grail said.

Vint saw disappointment cross over Hailey's face and sorrow filled him. She wanted to have it all, and that would mean he couldn't.

"What the hell would you even do with it, Hailey?" Kathy demanded. "You are going to live here? Make tea and sell it to those idiots who are trying to steal from us now?"

Hailey lifted her chin. "If Grandma could do it, why couldn't I? I know how to garden and collect herbs. I helped her every day we lived here and many after I moved out, way more than you ever did. I learned at her side."

"Oh right, great idea except maybe not, because the first recipe you tried was such a disaster!" Kathy jabbed a finger at Grail.

"Hardly a disaster, he is just ... here," Hailey defended weakly. "No harm done."

"He's a *demon*! You accidentally summoned a fucking demon, Hailey. He could crush you, eat you, anything, and probably make you think it was your idea."

"So? He may have those powers but all he's done is support me in wanting to make an informed decision which is more than I can say about you. And besides, if demons are so terrible you should be happy to keep the magic and not let Vint have it. Let's not forget that Grandma raised two half-demon children who are grieving here too and waiting for a decision that affects them. This isn't just about you and me anymore."

Kathy looked at Vint, a hint of guilt in her eyes. "All I know, is that bills have to be paid, you need a new job, and we can't afford the upkeep of this place. I already had a talk with the bank, Grandma had less than five thousand in there. We have to pay the rest of the funeral costs and then there will be nothing. We don't have a choice, Hailey." Kathy's tone softened and she crossed the room to her sister. "I already met with a realtor, she said that we could likely sell this place fast, especially if we let it go furnished. Then we can split the money. You'll be able to keep your apartment and have a cushion until you find a different job." She pushed a lock of hair behind Hailey's ear, just like she'd done when they were children. "Think about your future and what you can really handle. The stress of trying to make and sell tea? To make enough money to live on? I just think it would be too much."

"Too much," Hailey whispered. "Because I'm so delicate and I should just get another hotel job maybe, another desk job with idiots complaining about everything." She shook her head. "I am done with that, I'm capable of so much more," Hailey said, tears glistening in her eyes.

Kathy hugged her. "I know, I know you are, and you can go back to school, you can do whatever you want. You know Summer and I will support you in any way we can."

Hailey pushed her sister away and shook her head. "Any way you can, as long as I am doing what you think is right. What *you* think I can handle. Support me as long as it means you still have the ability to do what you really want?"

"No, Hailey I—"

Hailey held up a hand and stopped her sister's words. "I get it, you have a great life and you don't want anything to derail that trajectory. But I have nothing. I have been stagnant for a long damn time. This—" Hailey waved a hand around. "This is what I was waiting for, I can feel it. The twist in my gut, the anxiety that Grandma always told me to trust, it's still there but it's different. It's as if I can understand what my gut is telling me, good or bad, it doesn't just feel like impending doom and it's telling me that I am in the right place, that the magic is comforting, and I am more than you think I am." Hailey's voice broke and fresh tears raced down her face.

Kathy opened her mouth to speak then shut it and shook her head, embracing her sister.

"Kathy, Hailey, you both are grieving, and making decisions in the middle of that is just not good," Summer pointed out. "Let's all take a break from the conversation. Nothing has to be decided tonight."

"Taking your time is a good idea," Grail agreed.

Vint rolled his eyes at his father's input, designed to give him more time in this realm.

"You're right," Kathy said, turning to her girlfriend and smiling. "Let's make dinner."

Hailey didn't move as the two women walked out of the room. Once they were out, she turned her eyes on Vint and he saw a storm brewing there. He had a feeling it wasn't going to go his way, but at least she wasn't crying anymore.

"Grab a basket, we need to do some gathering out in the garden," Vint said, hoping to distract her.

CHAPTER

FOURTEEN

Hailey was seething as she walked around the garden and plucked and pruned just like her grandmother had taught her. She knew what all these plants were, not necessarily what they were used for, but she could learn. She knew how to properly prep them to be dried, how long to dry them and where. She'd paid attention by her grandmother's side while Kathy had read and drawn and spent time with friends.

And Kathy thought she knew what was best for Hailey.

First, Kathy had answered her phone. She said it was an accident but Hailey knew the woman had zero boundaries when it came to Hailey's life. And she'd been more than willing to ask Hailey's boss about how much time off she was going to have while they settled the estate, which led to him telling her none. Hailey was no longer employed. Then Kathy had dropped those bombs about her bills, her rent, Grandma's bank account and the realtor! What the hell was her deal? Why did she think she was in control of everything? Just because Kathy thought she had her life together so perfectly, just because she'd always seen her little sister as a screwup.

"You're bruising the petals," Vint said as she aggressively gathered.

"How long do we have to decide?" she asked him.

"Technically forever; realistically ... how long until your sister has a complete meltdown?"

"I think we have a day at most," she grumbled.

Vint laughed and the sound tingled down Hailey's spine.

"She's not wrong about some things, and that makes it all so much harder I just ... I just don't know, you know? I feel like I'm where I should be," she said guiltily. "I know what I agreed to before Grandma died, but everything's changed, why can't she see that?"

Vint gave her a half smile. "I get it, believe me. I feel good here too, this place is magical," he laughed again. "And I don't just mean that literally. Your grandmother made this place somewhere safe for my sister and I, it's special."

"Hey," Hailey said suddenly, turning to him with an idea rushing through her. "Help me."

"Help you what?" Vint said cautiously.

"Help me convince Kathy that I can do this. I can take on the magic and the house. Hell, maybe I can even sell tea like Grandma did, apparently it made her enough money. I might still have to get another job to supplement, but that's okay."

"And this would be a good deal for me because?" Vint asked, arms crossed over his chest.

Hailey bit her lip and looked the half-demon in the eye knowing she was asking him to help her keep the magic from him. "Because it's what she wanted, otherwise she would have bequeathed it all to you right from the start. She wanted Kathy and I to have it and maybe there's some other way I can help you? Maybe there's something I can do for you that will make your life easier too?"

Vint's eyes flicked down her body quickly then back to her face, pausing for a moment where she bit her lip nervously.

It was all so fast Hailey wasn't sure she'd actually seen what she thought she saw, but there was a new heat in his gaze and it flared something to life in her stomach as he met her eyes. What if he asked to sleep with her? What if he wanted sexual favors in return for being on her side?

What if she liked that idea way the fuck too much?

"I would owe you one," she said, a bit breathless.

His eyes darkened and he grabbed her arm in a firm grasp. "Never, say that to a demon."

Hailey felt a spike of fear like an icy finger of terror rush through her body. She wasn't sure if it was a reaction to his stern words or something emanating from his grip but she couldn't speak, only nod.

"There's nothing you can do to help a half-demon, Hailey," he said angrily and stalked away.

Hailey watched him go with her mouth hanging open and a sense of loss for something she had no right to desire. Not from him.

She turned back to the plants, mindlessly picking as she gathered herself back together, then slowly, she returned to the house.

Grail stood on the front porch as she approached. "Where are you headed?"

"Date. You don't seem to be about to come to any unanimous decisions tonight, so I am keeping my date with a pretty little blonde I met today."

"Seriously?"

"Deadly," he said. "I will be back to take a shift of watch for the night."

She watched him walk away with a hanging jaw. Some unsuspecting human was about to have a wild date with a demon. Hailey wasn't sure if she felt sorry for the woman or a twinge of jealousy. Not that she wanted to date Grail, but she hadn't been on a wild date with anyone in a while.

"He won't harm her," Batal said behind her.

"That's good."

"Grail has a particular taste for human women. He is one of the most frequently called upon by witches for a night even though he isn't a sex demon," Batal added as if it were no big deal.

Hailey tried to wrap her head around that but the image of Grail as some kind of demon call boy had her wanting to bleach her brain.

"Thanks for telling me, I guess."

Batal laughed. "You looked concerned."

"You know a lot about the demons," she said, turning to look at him.

"I do."

"Can you tell me what happens when you owe one a favor?"

"Oh, yeah, that's a big deal for demons. If you owe one a favor then they can call it up any time. The bridge between the demon realm and this world has a permanent bridge for them until the favor is repaid."

"So they wouldn't have a real reason to call it in," she pointed out.

"No, they would hold onto it as long as possible," he agreed. "But in that time, they could cause a lot of havoc for the humans and witches. Most full demons aren't as likeable as Grail."

Hailey shivered at the thought of a demon like Grail in his inhuman form wreaking havoc on the community whenever he felt like it.

"But keep in mind, he's still a demon, you still can't trust him. At his base, he is selfish and would do anything to get what he wants," Batal said, then turned and walked into the house.

She wanted to ask if that same warning applied to Vint, but she was afraid the answer would be *yes*.

Dinner was uncomfortable. Kathy and Summer made a great meal, and everyone enjoyed it, but Hailey refused to speak to either of them and Gina filled the silence by talking on and on about the trips she'd taken. When dinner was over the ghost maids, Valerie and Sarah, cleared the dishes.

"That's something I could get used to," Summer said with a smile.

"Literally could if you wanted my sister to keep the magic," Hailey snarked.

Summer's cheeks heated and she looked away.

"How about a drink and a game?" Kathy suggested.

"Oh, I love games," Gina declared, and Batal agreed quickly.

"I'll get the cards," Kathy said.

"I'll grab more wine," Vint offered.

Gina and Batal headed into the living room and Hailey was left with Summer.

"Are you afraid of the magic?" Hailey asked.

"What? No," Summer said with a bit of shock to her tone. "I am surprised, my whole idea of the world turned upside down," she laughed. "But it isn't scary, it just, is, I guess, and it somehow fits perfectly with what I knew of your grandmother."

Hailey nodded. "Yeah, I get what you're saying. It was like, once I knew, I wasn't that surprised after the initial shock. I was like, okay, yeah, this is what is out there and this is what Grandma was doing."

"It's weird, but really cool too," Summer said with a genuine smile.

"So you wouldn't leave my sister if she kept the magic?"

"God no, what kind of bitch do you think I am?" Summer

snapped. "I love Kathy. I wouldn't leave her for anything, but Hailey, this isn't about me, this isn't my choice to make. I'm just here to support Kathy through it, and you too of course. I love you like my own sister."

"I know, I just had to ask."

Summer crossed the room and wrapped Hailey in a warm embrace. "I get it. I am trying to stay out of it, honestly. I want you both to feel good about whatever you decide."

Hailey was comforted by that assurance. "My sister has always been very level-headed; I am sure that it's difficult for her to even consider embracing something this extraordinary."

"Oh yeah, she's barely holding her shit together," Summer said with a laugh. "Just keep that in mind, okay, she needs more time than you to process big changes."

Vint sat close to his sister as they drank wine and played crazy eights. Gina was cheating, he watched over her shoulder as she changed the cards in her hand. But he changed them back when she was distracted so she only won most of the time instead of every round.

Hailey glared at them and he wondered if she was sensing the magic he was using. Did she think he was cheating too?

He couldn't help lifting an eyebrow at her as if daring her to accuse him as he set down his second eight of the round.

"Fucking demons," Batal snapped then shot an apologetic look in Gina's direction. But she wasn't paying attention to him, she was currently trying to change Summer's cards while the woman was running to the kitchen to make popcorn.

Vint elbowed Gina while Batal played his card and then it was Hailey's turn.

"Are you sure this is the only game you know how to play," Hailey asked Gina.

"It's the best! Who would want to play anything else with cards?"

Hailey rolled her eyes and drew card after card without anything playable.

Vint coughed and turned the next card into an eight, loving the way Hailey's eyes lit up as she played it with a flourish. Her genuine smile and wide eyes made his body react, and not just with the desire to possess her body, but a true desire to see that smile more, to make her look at him with such genuine happiness, to be warmed by it.

In the middle of their second bottle of wine a knock on the door had everyone frozen for a moment, staring at each other. The spell of fun, the air of relaxed interaction was breaking and Vint desperately wanted to pull it back but then another knock came.

Drandy appeared. "Ma'ams there is a young woman at the door, would you like me to let her in?"

"No," Vint said quickly, and hurried to the door. Everyone followed.

He opened the door, using his body to shield the others from whatever was going to be there. It was unlikely to be a friendly visit at this time of night. Batal was right behind him, offering additional protection with his small body and Vint appreciated that. They both knew that the women in the house, aside from Gina, couldn't protect themselves.

One look at the young woman weeping on the porch had the men instinctively backing away. This wasn't at all what he'd feared, but in a way it could be worse. This woman reeked of desperate need. She looked a little older than Hailey and even the sight of his demon horns didn't cause her more than a slight widening of her eyes, She just stood there wringing her hands and bouncing lightly on her feet as if she were caught between fleeing and approaching.

"I need to speak with the sisters," she whispered in a trembling voice.

"What are you doing here?" Vint demanded.

"I'm not here to speak with demons," she said, voice a little stronger now that she had a clear view of Hailey and Kathy.

Vint wasn't letting her in though and Batal still stood close as well, ready to keep this witch out if they needed to.

"Who are you and what exactly are you here for?" Hailey asked, voice stern and Vint couldn't help feeling just a tinge of satisfaction that she'd taken offense to the weeping woman's treatment of him.

"I'm Joanna. I need your help. It's my son. He's so sick and —" her voice cracked, fresh tears started streaming down her face.

Hailey pushed past Vint and Batal to embrace Joanna and lead her inside. There was no way she was faking those emotions, whatever this was, it wasn't another coven trick. But that only eased a portion of what bothered Vint about this scenario and he met Gina's gaze as everyone else followed Hailey and Joanna to the living room.

"She's drawn to help," Gina said with a half smile.

"Yeah," Vint agreed then put his arm around his sister. He wanted to help too, he just wasn't so interested in helping witches who had treated him and his sister like shit all their lives.

They walked into the living room as Batal handed Joanna a glass of wine. "Here," Batal said as Hailey settled her onto the couch.

"Thanks," Joanna said between sobs then downed the whole thing.

"Can you start over? What are you here for?" Hailey prompted when she handed Batal the empty glass.

Joanna blinked rapidly at Hailey. "My son is sick. He was born with some health problems, but he'd been getting better with Merry's help and I ran out of the tea a couple days ago. Tonight he collapsed and he's having trouble breathing. I didn't know where else to go."

"I think you should take him to the hospital," Kathy said and Summer nodded agreement.

Vint liked that idea a lot and would even offer to drive, but the woman immediately discarded the possibility.

"No, we've tried that, we tried that so many times and they don't help, can't help. Whatever he has, they aren't able to fix it. The only thing that seems to make him feel better is Merry's tea," she pleaded, looking from Kathy to Hailey.

Hailey looked at him and he could see it all play out on her face. Her instincts were prompting her to help this woman, to take control of this situation. She looked back at Joanna. "Okay, I'm sure that's not a problem, do you know what was in it?"

"No, she never shared her recipes with anyone." Joanna's lips twisted with the statement. She may have come here looking for help, but she didn't like that she had to.

"Of course." Hailey looked at Vint again. He knew what she wanted and a part of him wanted to deny it, to say no way and stand between her and realizing how much good she could do with the magic. But he couldn't, and not because of the weeping witch on the couch. Because of Hailey, the look on her face, the hope and determination he saw there. He'd do anything to keep her feeling like she was finally in control of something in her life, to help her discover that she was able and talented and smart, all the things Kathy seemed determined to keep her from.

He hated it, but he nodded and darted out of the house to get the book because destroying Hailey's happiness was starting to weigh heavier than the loss of the magic.

Hailey's heart broke for Joanna and she gripped her hands but the woman pulled away and Hailey sat back on her heels. "We'll make it, don't worry, okay? We will make sure your son is alright."

Joanna burst into fresh tears and reached into her pocket and pulled out a wad of cash.

"Oh no, you don't have to—" Hailey said.

"Yes," Joanna said firmly. "I do."

"If she doesn't pay, it's a favor, and witches don't take favors from the likes of us or anyone associated with us," Gina said dryly.

"Oh," Hailey said quietly and took the money with a frown. This wasn't a friendly interaction; this was a business deal.

Did it matter to her? She still wanted to help, would never let a child suffer just to save her pride.

Summer chatted with Joanna while they waited, apparently they'd gone to school together and Hailey was glad that she wasn't expected to carry a conversation right then, she had too many contradictory thoughts and feelings. She glanced at Kathy who sat listening with a pensive look on her face. Hailey would give anything to know what her sister thought of all this, but now was not the time to ask. She didn't want to give Joanna any ammunition to take back to the coven. Even if she was here for her son, Hailey didn't doubt that she'd tell the coven what happened, what was said here, and Hailey couldn't risk her vulnerabilities becoming fodder for them.

When Vint arrived back with the book he followed Hailey into the kitchen while the others stayed with Joanna.

"How am I supposed to even know which tea to make?" Hailey asked, feeling a little desperate, sure that a little boy's life was on the line.

"Ask the book," Vint said.

"Ask the book?"

"It's a sentient entity, ask it," he said again.

Hailey took a breath and set the book on the counter softly. She looked down at it, so familiar and yet, somehow so much different than she remembered. "What tea do I make for Joanna's little boy?"

She stared with breath held as the book did absolutely nothing. She turned a glare on Vint.

He rolled his eyes. "You have to put some power and intention behind the request."

"I don't know how to do that," Hailey said, feeling a bit desperate.

Vint put a hand on her lower back and the heat of his touch spread throughout her lower body lightning fast, distracting her from her worry. "Just think about what you want as you ask and allow the magic to work through you. The magic is all around us, just let it in a little." His face was so close she felt his breath breeze by her cheek and his body was almost touching her side, close enough she could sense—even if not feel—him there and his smell filled her nostrils. It was all very distracting.

Hailey nodded and sucked in a breath, trying to tamp down

on the swirling desire that was coming to life in her. Maybe she shouldn't have had so much wine. "Step away, so I can concentrate," she said, and he gave a dark chuckle before moving back a pace.

She cleared her mind and shook her body then concentrated on what she wanted, which was to help a little boy who was sick. She felt a warm tingle reach into her mind as she thought about her goal. It was soft and unsure, as if it was expecting to be kicked back out of her mind but she welcomed it and more poured in. She closed her eyes and let the feeling of it run through her body. When she felt like she couldn't possibly take any more she opened her eyes and looked at the book again. It was different. The cover was glowing with a purple light. She gasped at the beauty of it, the raw draw it had for her, she wanted to reach out and grasp it, hold it close and read every page. Absorb every bit of knowledge it held but somehow, she also knew that was impossible because the knowledge within was constantly growing and expanding.

"This book is linked to others," she whispered.

"It's likely that this grimoire is linked with other grimoires from the same family line," Vint confirmed.

That thought fascinated her but now was not the time to wonder about it, she had a task, an important one. "What tea can save Joanna's boy?" she asked the book, her voice low and husky. Then she reached out and opened it, flipping through pages until she came to one that she just knew was what she needed. Without taking even a moment to second guess herself she started reaching for the ingredients, measuring and crushing until she was done.

When she turned from the counter with a jar of tea in hand, she felt something that she wasn't sure she'd ever felt in her life. Purpose, drive, and completion. Every part of what she'd just done felt like what her life was supposed to be.

And when Vint saw the look on her face his own became guarded and she knew he was seeing what she felt, knew he was seeing her real desire to have this magic rather than giving it to him.

Her gut clenched with guilt.

"Come on. Joanna's boy is waiting," he said.

That night as Hailey stared up at the familiar ceiling of her teenage bedroom she thought about the energy she'd felt in the kitchen earlier. She wished she could describe it to Kathy, make her sister understand how fulfilling and right it had been to embrace the magic and do a spell to help someone who needed her, as though a piece of herself had clicked into place. Never in her life had she had the experience of helping someone in need like that. The closest she'd ever come was when a guest at the hotel ran out of toilet paper and called down to the front desk in embarrassed desperation. But this was different—important. Hailey knew her sister wasn't interested in hearing it though, Kathy's mind was made up.

Hailey rolled over and stared out at the dark night, enjoying the gentle breeze coming in the open window. She felt safe knowing Batal and Gina were out there watching things. They'd volunteered to take the first watch, no one wanted to leave the house completely vulnerable all night, so they were sleeping in shifts. Well, the demons were. Kathy, Summer and Hailey were supposed to be getting a good night's rest seeing as they were a more delicate species. So far, all Hailey had done was stare and think, wondering if she was going to be forced to give up the one thing that finally felt right about her life.

Frustrated with her inability to sleep, she slipped out of bed, threw on a sweater and wandered downstairs in her frog pajama shorts and fuzzy socks. After Joanna's visit she'd asked

Vint not to take the book back, instead they were hiding it in the oven again so she pulled it out and sat at the table.

"Can I get you anything, Ma'am?" Valerie asked, appearing beside her.

"No, um, go to bed?" she said, unsure if ghosts did that. Valerie just smiled and nodded then disappeared again.

Hailey tucked her legs up on the chair and opened the book. There was no purple glow or swirl of power, but she felt a hum of recognition in the book as she touched it, as if it were anticipating her needing it again and it was happy to have her peruse its pages.

"Can't sleep?" Grail asked, coming into the room looking a little drunk and a little disheveled, apparently his date had gone all the way.

"No," she said with a sigh. "You look like you could use some sleep though."

He nodded and took the seat across from her. "The book likes you," he said.

"Oh," she smiled down at it. "Yeah, I think it does."

"You don't have to keep the magic to keep the book."

"I know, but then it's just recipes, right?"

"Mostly, yeah, but even with magic it won't solve your financial issues."

"No, I suppose it won't," she agreed, annoyed that everyone knew about her money and job troubles. But then she thought of the cash Joanna had handed her and wondered if the book would. Not that her sister would agree that making tea for a living and selling it out of her living room was a good enough career choice to make.

"What's that face about?" Grail asked.

"My sister, she thinks I need to be more responsible, make decisions that will secure my future. Mostly she wants me to make decisions that she agrees with."

Grail nodded but his face was blank. "Makes sense, Kathy is a very smart woman."

"So you think I should give up the magic, let Vint have it? Would you find him a more acceptable son if he had more power?"

"No, Vint will never be a full demon. He's a very good half-demon though," Grail admitted and then looked a little surprised he'd said that. "I think you should keep the magic and I think you should use it for whatever makes you feel good. I'm a demon, remember. I am all about what makes you feel good, not what makes other people happy."

Hailey shook her head. "What does it say about me that I want to take the advice of a demon over my own sister?"

Grail grinned wide. "Tells me that you are the perfect candidate to continue doing what Merry started. She's the only witch I've ever met who would do what she did for those two kids. Half-demons are abandoned by their covens, left to fend for themselves, they grow up alone and scared, and if they find their way into the demon realm, they are used as nothing better than slaves and servants. Merry saved their lives. She was a good woman, a great witch."

"Is that why Gina travels so much?" Was Gina without a place to land, did she not fit anywhere? Hailey's heart went out to the girl.

Grail nodded.

"Goodnight, Grail," Hailey said, taking the book upstairs with her. If she couldn't sleep, she'd read.

Vint walked into the kitchen after Hailey went upstairs. He'd caught the end of their conversation but had hesitated to interrupt. He was feeling things for Hailey, things that made him second guess his desire to take the magic away from her. But he needed it, he could do good with it.

"Why did you tell her that?" Vint demanded.

"Tell her what?" Grail said with an innocent look on his face.

"You aren't supposed to be encouraging her in any certain direction."

"Is that what I did?" Grail defended.

"You told her that she should take it and continue in Merry's footsteps."

"I did, and I also told her what a horrible life you half-demons have. Do you think she'll take something from you that could improve your life and Gina's?"

Vint opened his mouth, then shut it. Damn, tricky bastard.

"I'm off to get a few winks. Wake me up when it's my turn to watch for witchy invaders. You know, I don't think Hailey is going to be sleeping any time soon. She seemed mighty distracted when she walked out of here." Grail winked and sauntered out of the room.

Vint glared at his father's retreating back, wondering what his game was. But his words swirled around in Vint's mind until he found himself walking up to Hailey's room unsure of his intention.

He knocked quietly on the door so if she was asleep she wouldn't be disturbed. A moment later he heard her footsteps and the door opened.

"Is everything alright?" she asked. Damn she was cute, hair in a ponytail, dressed in soft shorts with little frogs on them and matching tank top. He wanted to wrap her in his arms and cuddle her, to breathe in her scent and hear her soft voice as she talked about literally anything.

"Grail said you'd grabbed the book and I thought if you

were reading you must not be able to sleep and might want company."

"Oh, sure," she said, holding the door open wide in invitation.

Vint walked in and settled on the windowsill trying to think of a valid reason for disturbing her peace at this hour. Hailey sat in the middle of the bed, feet tucked under her and the book open where she'd apparently been reading. He tried not to stare at the low neckline of her top and how obvious it was she wasn't wearing a bra by the way her nipples pressed against the thin fabric. His mouth went dry and he was momentarily struck dumb, not a thought in his head that didn't revolve around what it would feel like to run his hand under the thin strap and let it fall over her shoulder, how it would reveal more of her silky skin but likely stop just before revealing that most precious bud he ached to wrap his lips around.

She shifted uncomfortably, pulling on a sweater she had laying on the bed next to her and looking at Vint like the worst kind of lecherous beast for the way he was staring. He cleared his throat and looked behind him out the window.

"I was just looking over recipes. Trying to see if I could discern what they were for," Hailey said bringing his gaze back to her. "This one here is called *Sleep*, so that's obvious," she laughed and turned the page. "This is almost the same but for one small change, see, she adds in honeysuckle and it's called, *Wedding Tea*." She sighed deeply. "I wish Grandma was here to explain it all."

"The magic is all you need, trust that, then you'll sense what the recipes are for, what's right for different situations. It's meant to be vague, so that anyone else reading it won't be able to understand."

"I guess that makes sense, wouldn't want a human to make something terrible appear," Hailey gave a little laugh.

Vint shook his head. "No, it's not a safeguard against humans, but witches. A human could make any of those teas and nothing would happen, but witches, they can add the necessary power to make the spell. Without your grandmother's magic—the Honeycomb magic—the spells remain mysterious. Another witch would be taking a huge risk making any of those."

Hailey gave a weary sigh. "Her magic, the book of recipes, or spells I guess, it's a huge legacy and responsibility. It's a lot." She met his gaze and her eyes showed all the worry and fear that she was trying to hold back.

What else could he say. "It is."

She bit her lip and his eyes were stuck there, wondering what they tasted like.

"Vint I—" she looked away and mumbled. "I wonder if Gina and Batal are doing okay on their lookout."

Vint would have given anything to know what she'd been about to say, but he also realized she was right to lighten the mood. He shouldn't be staring at her like a lecherous demon. "Right now I'm just worried about Batal and what Gina might be making him do to earn those treats she bought today."

Hailey laughed and the sound was an aphrodisiac, his body, already primed to respond to her, reacted and he wanted to hear her do that again and again for the rest of his life. The thought struck him like a slap to the face and he pushed it away, far too real and raw.

"Batal is so in love with her it's ridiculous," Hailey said with a final snort laugh. "It's cute really and I'm sure whatever they do for those treats is consensual."

Vint shrugged. "I guess, until she leaves again, and he's depressed for months."

He could see the sadness sweep over Hailey's face for the heartbreak of a man she barely knew. She was a deep feeler, a generous soul, and a part of him, the demon part, knew he could use that to his advantage.

He hated himself, even as he pushed the advantage he saw. "If I had the power to, I would make this a safe haven, not just for her and me, but any other half-demon out there that wanted it," he said as if it were an offhand remark without forethought. He knew he needed to pad the idea with things she wouldn't think she could do. "I could ward the place against the witches and put up a shield good enough to hide our activities from them and the humans. We could just be ourselves here. I could welcome other supernaturals too, like Batal, who are homeless roamers in a world run by witches and humans. There aren't a lot of safe places for the magically inclined who don't fit in their little box."

"That sounds nice," Hailey said quietly.

Vint cleared his throat, guilt crawling up from his stomach. "Well, I think I better go get a little rest before my shift. See you in the morning, Hailey."

"Yeah," she said a little absently, as she stared down at the closed book.

Vint closed her door behind him and sagged against it. Fighting the urge to go back in and apologize. He needed that power, and he had to do whatever it took to get it.

He made his way to the living room and laid down on the couch, but sleep wasn't coming and he ended up staring at the ceiling with images of her rushing through his mind until Gina and Batal came in giggling. Batal was wearing a headband with cat ears and Gina had a ball of yarn in her hand, her eyes twinkling with mischief.

He didn't want to know.

"It's your turn, we are off to bed," Gina said.

Vint sat up and rubbed his face. "Did you see anything?"

"The magic-eaters came and went, they must have

remembered there was magic here but they couldn't sense it, so they left quickly. You set a good barrier," Batal said.

"Yeah, that's an easy one."

"Not for me," Gina griped.

"Aw, babe you have so many other talents," Batal crooned.

"Be a good boy and I'll show you a few," Gina answered.

Batal meowed at her and she giggled, patting his head.

Vint rolled his eyes, hopping up. "I'll be on the porch."

He settled onto a comfortable chair there and watched the night. It was after midnight and way before any early birds would appear. He liked this time of day, when the world seemed to sleep and he could breathe easy.

"What was it you truly intended?" he asked aloud, as if Merry was going to appear beside him like she'd done so many times in his life. Even when the girls had lived here, and he and Gina were on their own he would come back at a time like this and sit in peace. She would sense him there and come out to chat, or just sit in companionable silence.

He missed her and he remembered how she used to talk of Hailey and Kathy.

"My granddaughters are something special you know. It's such a shame what their father forced me to do. They would have been great wielders of magic."

"Why not just teach them now? With their parents gone what's stopping you?"

"Honor mostly. I could get around any spell, even the one he bound me to in order to keep my mouth shut about the magic. But I would be breaking my word. A person's word is everything, Vint. I taught you that."

"You did," he agreed.

"When I'm gone perhaps," she'd said, eyeing him slyly. "Perhaps when I'm gone."

She hadn't clarified. One of the girls had a nightmare and

she'd rushed inside to comfort the child. Vint hadn't asked after that either, afraid to think that the magic he had come to think of as his own due inheritance would go to the girls instead. Untrained and clueless witches would get what he wanted.

And that is what he'd feared to know, so he hadn't asked. And now, he still wasn't sure.

"Watch them when I'm gone, they'll need a bit of guidance."

Those were the words that he'd heard from her on his last visit. She'd known she was getting sick, could sense the end near and she'd summoned him to give that last request. A request that had surprised him. She had never so bluntly implied that he should interact with Hailey and Kathy.

The next day Hailey was there, caring for her and she hadn't left once, hadn't given Vint a chance to go in and ask for more details.

Then Merry was gone and now it was too late to get answers, he could only go on what he knew.

His word was his honor and he'd promised to guide the women. He would obey her last request and make sure the coven got none of the magic no matter what.

But his demon side rebelled, said his words were just words and they could all be twisted to mean whatever he wanted after the fact. Maybe taking care and guiding Hailey and Kathy meant he needed the magic most.

Maybe he really could do the most good with it.

SIXTEEN

Hailey dreamed of her grandmother and woke feeling refreshed despite the early hour. She could hear birds chirping outside and the sun was bright, but the air coming through the open window was crisp with morning dew.

Something was tickling her brain, a remembered moment in the dream, but like dreams tend to, it was just outside her reach and taunted her with almost solidifying in her mind. She was left with a feeling that her grandmother was worried about their situation here but not why exactly.

She dressed and headed downstairs; the book tucked under her arm. She figured as long as she had it in hand, it was safe enough.

Gina was sitting on the kitchen counter when Hailey arrived, her bare feet swinging. She had a black silk robe on and by the way it gapped open Hailey could tell she was wearing not much else. Hailey was glad she'd pulled on some sweats and a sweatshirt before coming down. There were far too many people in the house to be that bare, but Gina didn't seem to care at all. Batal was standing at the stove in a pair of jeans and no shirt. His bare back rippling with muscles that somehow surprised Hailey due to his short stature. He was making pancakes, and Summer and Kathy were out on the sun porch sipping coffee. No sign of Grail or Vint.

"Morning, sunshine," Gina said brightly and smiled at Hailey.

"Morning," Hailey said and noticed Gina had what looked suspiciously like cat scratches on her inner thighs.

Batal looked over his shoulder and smiled. "You are up early too, seems like no one is resting well today except Vint."

"Oh?" she asked, trying not to sound too curious about the man.

"He's passed out on the couch," Gina said.

"And Grail?"

"Out front glaring at the coven members who just happen to be walking their dogs by the house since sunup this morning."

"Great," Hailey grumbled and poured a cup of coffee.

She decided she wasn't ready to talk to her sister so she went out front to see how scary Grail was being. She didn't want little kids to start spreading rumors about this house, turn it into a local legend of horror, though it might already be too late for that. She found him standing against a pillar on the steps, arms crossed over a bare chest, khaki shorts and hiking boots on. What was with everyone this morning, did no one think fully clothed before ten a.m. was a thing? He glared out at the street where there was no one currently passing.

"Sleep well?" she asked, sitting on the steps.

"Yes, until Vint woke me up for guard duty. Did you know that the coven walks by here every ten to twenty minutes with some dumb animal in tow as if it were their duty to watch every going on in this place?"

"I did not."

"Well they do, have been since sun came up and it's ridiculous."

"You are scaring them off it seems. No one came knocking and trying to deliver treats or steal the book," she said, tapping it in her lap.

"You shouldn't have that out here."

"If I keep it at hand, I know it's safe, feels right," she reasoned.

He just grunted.

"And besides, you'll protect me," she said with a grin.

He looked at her with a raised eyebrow briefly then back out to the street.

Hailey took a sip of her coffee. "You are bound by my summoning," she said with a dramatically deep voice.

Grail laughed. "True."

They stared out at the street for another minute and then a man she recognized came into view, it was Mr. Pentack who had approached her in the grocery store parking lot and threatened her yesterday. He was walking a small poodle and although he had some dark glasses on, she could feel his intense stare. His presence was unnerving—he was not a neighbor which meant the coven was coming from everywhere just to watch her house. What did they think they were going to gain from that, she wondered.

A rumble emitted from Grail's chest as Mr. Pentack drew closer but it didn't seem to stop the man from coming right up to the gate and pausing.

He pointed at Hailey. "You are making a big mistake, girl."

"So are you," Grail growled.

"No decisions have been made, move along," Hailey answered.

"You have a demon guard, housemates too. This is not what Merry would have wanted."

Hailey laughed. "Merry practically raised two of those demons so fuck you and your high horse," she snapped, and Mr. Pentack lifted his chin, turned away and walked along without another word.

Grail looked down at her with a half grin. "They all think you should be scared shitless like they are. They don't understand anyone who stops for a moment to know a demon, even a halfie."

"Maybe I am," Hailey grumbled into her cup.

Grail shrugged. "Maybe you are, but not for the reasons they presume you should be."

Hailey knew he was right. She had no fear of Grail or Vint or Gina. She feared losing her family's legacy and she feared not being able to help others that needed her family's kind of magic. Why couldn't Kathy understand the consequences of letting it all go?

And she feared keeping something from Vint that rightfully belonged to him. Would he walk away if she did, would she ever see the half-demon again?

That thought had her gut twisting.

Kathy and Summer stepped out onto the porch dressed for work and Hailey was glad for the interruption to her spiraling thoughts.

"We will be back this evening, and we need to make some real decisions," Kathy said with a heavy sigh. "Summer and I have our own life to live, pets, plants, and a home we love. We can't keep staying here but I know you won't go home ... if you even have a home much longer," she added stiffly. "We need to make a final call. Tonight." Kathy said firmly and in a tone Hailey recognized as one that she expected to be final and followed to the letter. She'd used it a thousand times with Hailey over the years, always the voice of reason and the one in charge.

Hailey didn't respond, what could she say? Kathy wasn't wrong, it was time to make decisions. She just knew she wasn't going to make the ones that Kathy wanted her to.

Summer gave Hailey a sympathetic look then took Kathy's hand and they walked down the path.

"Looks like time's almost up, I will make sure to enjoy today," Grail said.

"Carousing at the local dive bar again?" Hailey asked.

"As long as I'm not needed here," he said then held out his hand.

Hailey stared at it with a questioning eyebrow.

He rolled his eyes and wiggled his fingers.

Hailey stiffened but set her own hand in his. He put the other on top and pressed. She felt a sharp stick then he let her go.

"What the hell was that?" she hissed, looking intensely at her palm but seeing nothing.

"A calling mark. If you think about me, I'll know you need me." He grinned wide. "So don't think about me unless you really want me to show up," he winked.

She smiled at him. "You're nice, aren't you?"

His eyes darkened and his skin turned a shade of red that no human could claim even with the worst kind of sunburn. "No, I am not," he growled and walked into the house.

"I think you are," she whispered into her cup.

"Breakfast!" Batal called.

Vint woke up for breakfast and after they'd eaten, the ghost maids cleaned up.

Hailey took a breath to steady her nerves then faced Vint. "Vint, I want you to show me some magic."

"What do you mean?" he asked skeptically.

"I am already a little magic, right? That's why Kathy's jewelry is making Summer see the usually unseeable and why I can see the ghosts and why I could make the tea and summon your dad."

"Right, you have a natural inclination for magic because of your bloodline."

"Exactly, so I want you to help me do something cool with it. Something that I can do without even fully embracing the magical inheritance, can you do that?"

He looked like he was debating. "I think so."

"Of course you can!" Gina said excitedly. "You are gifted yourself because Grail is a magician."

"A what?" Hailey asked, confused. "I thought Grail was a demon." She looked down at her palm trying to not think too hard about the guy, she didn't need him to pop in and waste the emergency link. Was it a one time link, she wondered. She really should have asked more questions before letting him leave the house.

"He is, but there are different types of demons. Grail is what they call a magician because he is very magically inclined, almost like a witch but in demon form."

"What is your father like?" Hailey asked Gina.

"He is a sex demon," she said with a shrug.

Hailey nearly spit out her coffee at that casual admission. "A sex demon?"

Gina nodded. "Not very powerful in magic but great in bed."

"So you are half ... sex demon?" Hailey asked slowly.

"Yes, she is," Batal said with a purr.

"So I am not very magically inclined. I only got it from my mother's side, not both like Vint did," Gina explained.

Hailey shook her head and realized that it made a lot of sense.

"I'm glad I didn't accidentally summon *your* dad," she said.

Gina laughed, "Oh, you would have been done for. No

human or witch can resist him. But you would have enjoyed it, they always do."

"Until he leaves them a dried out husk desperate for more, not eating or sleeping and crying into their pillows about the lost love of their life," Vint snarled.

Gina's face sobered and the room fell silent. Hailey didn't have to ask, she suddenly knew that was what must have happened to their own mother, must have been the reason why they were left alone, and her grandmother had to take them in. She looked from Batal to Gina, the desperation clear in the way Batal acted around Gina. Was he lost in her powers too, would she destroy him? Was that why she wouldn't commit to him? Was she somehow trying to save him from her own powers?

"Let's do this outside," Vint said, thankfully changing the subject.

They ended up in the backyard where they were unlikely to be seen. "Okay, a simple spell even a baby witch can do is moving things around, so we will start with that."

"Like telekinesis?"

"Exactly. See that flower over there, the bluebell?"

Hailey nodded; eyes glued to the flower. She watched as it wobbled slightly then the stem broke, and it floated right to her.

She giggled as she grasped it. "That's amazing!"

Vint lifted one corner of his mouth. "The trick is simple; you just need to look at what you want to move and envision it doing what you want it to do. There should be a sort of magical build up in your body as you concentrate and then it should happen."

"Okay," she said, unsure but willing to try. She looked at a small rock on the ground not too far away and pictured it lifting straight up into the air. She narrowed her eyes at it and tensed her body, but nothing happened. "Damn," she hissed after a couple minutes of nothing, and a small sheen of sweat was on her forehead.

She felt Vint's hands on her shoulders, squeezing lightly. "You're too tense. You're trying too hard. Magic isn't hard, it should flow naturally."

"Easy for you to say," she hissed. "That rock didn't even budge."

He chuckled and the sound vibrated through her. "You need to relax a bit, concentrate but not like if it doesn't happen you'll die, more like a wish."

"A wish, okay."

She looked at the rock, she tensed her body and wished.

Vint's hands moved along her arms and his breath fanned her cheek. "Relax your muscles, you're using your magic, not physical strength here, Hailey."

Her body tingled at his closeness and his words. She wondered what it would feel like to have him pressed close to her, the full length of his body against her back in an embrace or dance rather than this almost close touch that was intended only as guidance.

Vint let out a surprised gasp as his body pressed to her.

Hailey yelped and spun around, one hand flying to her mouth in embarrassment mixed with joy. Had she done that?

Vint raised an eyebrow at her and gave a full smile. "I see you just needed to find something you really wanted."

Her cheeks burned and she covered her face with her hands. "I didn't ... I mean I wasn't ..."

He took pity on her and stepped back. "You got the magic to do what you wanted, that's great. Now, try it with the rock, just as relaxed and easy, a concentrated thought."

Hailey turned back to the rock; thankful he was being so casual about her blunder. This time when she looked at the rock and thought about it lifting, she tried to do it with a simple wishful thought. It wobbled and stilled but she didn't give up and a few minutes later she was lifting rocks with ease.

Vint gave her an approving nod. "I think you have that one down."

"Teach me something else," she said with a clap, she felt so powerful, so vibrant and she didn't want it to stop.

Vint spent hours with her, teaching her simple things. How to create a light with her hands, how to force a seed to grow and how to call up a small breeze. Every new spell she learned made her feel more powerful, more in tune with herself and way surer that she wanted the magic, that this was what her grandmother had meant for her.

And with every celebration she made of a new skill learned she saw a sadness and an acceptance in Vint's gaze.

Vint found Gina on the front porch drinking wine and waving cheerfully at the glaring coven members who walked by.

"You're teaching her," Gina said, no judgement in her voice, only curiosity.

"I am, it's what Merry asked me to do."

Gina nodded. "So you are going to accept that the magic is theirs?"

Vint knew his sister well, the question was posed in a casual fun way, the way she spoke of everything because she wanted nothing but fun and joy in her life. But there was the slightest hitch, the smallest quake, because she knew that the magic would have meant something to him, and to her by association. She had been hoping that Vint would take the magic and the home, and she would be able to live there safely once again.

"It's up to her, I can't take it from her, they have to decide," Vint said and put an arm around his sister. "You should come stay with me when this is done."

"In your dungeon of a home? No thanks, I think I'll head for the Bahamas, catch some sun and surfers," she said with a grin.

"What about Batal?" Vint asked. He cared for his friend, and he knew how much the cat man loved his sister but she toyed with him. Not only because of her natural inclination for making sex a game, but because she was afraid one person couldn't be enough for her, that she'd only destroy him in the end.

"You know he's better off without me," she said in an uncharacteristically somber tone.

Vint wasn't sure she was wrong. Demons, even half ones like them, caused a wake of destruction wherever they went. Hailey was better off without him as well, he wasn't what she needed on her journey of magic discovery.

"Aren't they all," he sighed. "I don't think I can really help Hailey much more than I already have."

Gina looked at him with surprise. "But you're the best at magic, even with limited power you've done amazing things."

"Demon things," he snarled. "She's going to need to learn witch magic, Gina. We can't help her with that, I don't know what Merry was thinking."

Vint stalked away, pissed that he cared, pissed that Merry had put him in this position and pissed that he wanted to be what Hailey needed.

Demons destroy, he reminded himself and Hailey wanted nothing more than to help and heal. He could see it in her, feel it in her magic. She was all goodness and light.

She was the opposite of him.

CHAPTER
SEVENTEEN

That afternoon Hailey was sitting in the sunroom with a cup of tea when Batal sauntered up to her in his cat form. She patted the seat beside her and he jumped up, turning a few times, then laying down. She petted him and he began to purr.

"What happens if Kathy and I never come to an agreement?" she wondered aloud.

Batal shifted to human form beside her, and she found herself for a moment awkwardly petting his thigh.

"Warn a girl," she said.

He just laughed. "I can't talk to you while in that form. You are the one who asked me a question."

"It was rhetorical, of course I didn't expect a cat to answer me."

He shrugged. "Well here I am anyway. If you two don't decide together I think the magic will sit idle. I don't think it will go away immediately, but it will eventually start to get annoyed, might start playing tricks because it's bored."

Hailey nodded, she was sure Vint had said something similar. "Unless someone steals it."

"Right, that's a real danger."

"The coven." Hailey wondered if there was a way to make peace with them.

"Or a demon," Batal added. "A roaming demon could capture it, use it to their own advantage with disastrous results."

"But demons don't usually roam, unless they're half-demons living in this realm."

"Usually," Batal agreed. "But it can happen and even a powerful half-demon could make a play for the power."

"So why doesn't Vint or Gina?"

"Even if they were that powerful, which they aren't. They loved Merry; they'd never do anything to disrespect her wishes."

"I guess I knew the answer to that one already," Hailey agreed.

"What kind of tea did you make there?"

"Green, just plain green tea, no accidental spells," she laughed.

"Staying safe, good plan. But you've been reading the book. Do you think you're understanding how your grandmother did her tea spells?"

"I think so, a little." Hailey shrugged, almost embarrassed to say that she understood anything, it felt like there was so much more to learn. She had no right to claim even the smallest bit of knowledge. "It would probably take years to be confident with all of them."

"You could have years," Batal pointed out.

"I could," she agreed. But would she? She wanted to ask Batal what he thought she should do but she assumed he'd side with Vint having the magic because it would benefit Gina. "Ouch," she hissed, a sudden sharp pain in her palm.

"What is it?" Batal asked, staring at her hand where she rubbed it.

"Nothing I just—" she hissed again as another sharp burn ripped through her palm. "What the fuck?"

Batal grabbed her hand and looked at it. Neither of them spoke as a black circle appeared out of nowhere.

"Who gave you a demon mark?" Batal demanded.

"Grail, in case I needed him while he was at the bar picking up women," she said weakly, knowing she'd been stupid to just accept the thing without any real explanation from the demon. "Why? What's happening?" She started to feel panicked. Her blood racing and her heart beating wildly. She took in sharp short breaths and stared wide-eyed at Batal hoping for answers.

"He's calling *you* for help," Batal said between clenched teeth.

This had to be bad. Hailey wanted to curl into a ball, she wanted to hide but the burning in her palm wasn't easing. She didn't know what to do so she was frozen.

"Ouch!" she yelled as another sharp pain sliced through her palm.

Vint ran into the room followed by Gina.

"What's going on?" Vint snarled. His eyes were bright with fury and his fists were clenched. She'd never seen him look so demonic and somehow it was comforting instead of frightening seeing him as such a powerful force, and knowing he was on her side. She felt her anxiety ease and her paralysis let go.

Hailey held up her palm.

"Grail is in trouble," Batal said.

Vint's lips thinned, and he narrowed his eyes at Hailey. "What did you do?"

"Nothing, I—I don't know, is this bad?" Her voice betrayed her panic and she wanted to cry.

"You can't trust a demon, Hailey," Vint snapped. "If he's in danger he's going to draw on your power to save himself. He'll always put himself first."

"O-okay," she stuttered trying to remain calm while her heartbeat stayed elevated, and her blood continued rushing through her and pounded in her ears. "That's okay, right?" she pleaded, unable to hold back a couple tears.

"Until there's nothing left if he has to," Gina added.

Hailey's eyes widened with understanding. This could kill her, she needed to get her shit together. She stood quickly and her head swam. She wobbled slightly and Vint caught her arm.

"Fuck, let's go. Where the hell is he?" Vint demanded.

"I don't know," Hailey said.

"You do, you just need to calm down enough to feel it," Vint instructed. He turned her to face him and put his hands on her face. "Look at me, Hailey, I want you to focus on my words and breathing. I need you to match my breathing." He spoke slowly and his warm hands stayed on her face, keeping her where he wanted her.

Hailey reached up and put her hands on his chest, feeling the rise and fall. She concentrated on that feeling and slowly, her own breathing started to match his. She stared into his dark eyes and saw worry, fear, and anger. She softened as she realized that those emotions were for her, for her safety and what Grail could do to her.

"Good girl," Vint said softly. "Now I want you to tell me, where is Grail?"

Hailey shuddered at his words so silky and soft, his breath hot on her skin, so close to her face. But she did as he asked. She felt Grail and she thought she did know where he was, she had a sense at least.

Vint must have seen it in her eyes when she made the connection because he smiled, one of his rare full smiles that made her want to do anything to keep it there. "Let's go kick his ass," Vint said.

Hailey directed them to a bar in town and when they pulled up it looked deserted, no cars parked in the lot despite the lit up open sign. Hailey had been in the place once or twice. It was a good spot to drink when she didn't want to be blasted by too loud live music but a game of pool and a jukebox was more the scene. Many of the usual patrons were of the 'drink all day' sort, and older than her by at least twenty years.

But the beer tasted the same and was cheaper than the party all night young crowd on the main strip of downtown, places close to the hotel she no longer worked at.

They all jumped out of Vint's truck and stared at the front of the building, unsure.

"What do you think is going on in there?" Hailey asked, it was silent out there in a way that felt unnatural and made her shiver. Vint put an arm around her, offering warmth and she didn't hesitate to lean into his warm body.

"It's nothing good if you're still feeling a pull. You should wait out here," Vint instructed.

"Fuck that," she snapped and pulled away from him, sauntering forward as if her heart wasn't beating a million miles an hour and she wasn't about to throw up from nerves. If whatever this was had the potential of killing her, she was not going to sit back and wait to see what happened.

Vint was right at her side, Gina and Batal close behind them. She appreciated that none of them argued, they didn't try and tell her she couldn't handle it. They treated her like an adult who could make her own damn decisions. And that did a lot to ease the knot of tension in her body.

Vint opened the old wooden door. Inside Hailey could see the unnatural glow of light from a dozen neon beer signs. Vint stepped in, staying in front of her, stopping just inside and blocking her from whatever was in the dim room. Hailey had to push him in order to get a view of what was going on, why Grail had called her here.

The place looked empty aside from Grail sitting at the bar, a young and pretty bartender behind the bar looking like she had been crying, and a very ugly demon standing next to Grail with a drink in his hand.

The new demon was grey skinned with large yellow eyes that had slitted black pupils. His mouth and jaw were shaped in such a way that it made her certain he had teeth in there she would *not* want to see. Bright white hair stuck out all around his head and two pearlescent horns stood straight up at least six inches above the unruly strands. He was dressed in a white robe that reached the floor and the whole effect was very frightening; no wonder the trembling bartender was in tears.

"Belinzar," Vint sneered. "What the hell are you doing here?"

"I called him." A man stood up from a table in a dark corner surprising Hailey. He walked forward, sipping a drink, and Hailey recognized him immediately. Fucking Mr. Pentack. "I told you that you would regret not siding with me, Hailey."

She glared at the man even as a new wave of anxiety and fear raced through her body. "I didn't think the coven was into demons. Isn't that why you all shunned my grandmother?"

"Yes, the coven does tend to look poorly on those of us who would dabble with the creatures of the demon realm."

"You aren't part of the coven?" she asked, unable to hide her surprise.

"Oh no, they kicked me out long ago, but you see, unlike your grandmother, I didn't have anything worthwhile to them. I didn't get to keep a reluctant bond with them, I was just ostracized completely." The man's eyes flashed with anger and in response his demon friend seemed to pulse with energy.

"Okay …" Hailey said, trying to figure out what this madman rant was going to lead to. "So what exactly are you after here? You want us to be friends?"

He laughed viciously. "I want Merry's power."

Of course, why did she even ask?

Vint laughed and the man snarled at him. The demons at the bar just drank quietly, observing the interactions and the poor bartender sniffled.

"She left it to me," Vint said, crossing his arms over his chest.

"So I hear, but only if *she* doesn't decide to keep it? Her and her sister. So it isn't yours, is it? It's no ones. Which means it could be mine! Unclaimed magic is just sitting there waiting for a worthy host."

Hailey met Vint's gaze and she saw real fear there that had her own ratcheting up.

"It's not that easy," Vint said, his voice somehow still calm. "Otherwise you wouldn't have called in reinforcements."

"It might be easy enough if I take out a few obstacles."

Icy fear filled Hailey.

"You won't be killing Hailey. I am here to see to it she's safe until she makes a decision," Grail said in an almost bored tone. He was lounging against the bar as if he couldn't possibly be more relaxed about the situation, but something told her it was an act. Her palm was burning and when she met his gaze he flicked his eyes to the demon beside him.

He was clearly trying to communicate with her, but she had no idea what it was he wanted her to know—or do. She knew next to nothing about demons and she was pretty sure that other than the bartender, she was the most vulnerable being in the room.

"Well, it sounds like we have some things to hash out, why

don't you come by the house tonight and we can all talk," Batal suggested with a friendly smile.

"Sure thing, but not with your demon bodyguard," Mr. Pentack said with a wicked grin. "Belinzar, take him out."

Belinzar moved fast, but so did Grail. The two demons faced off. Grail shed his human form and was once again the terrifying red beast she'd seen originally. He was larger than Belinzar in this form but they were equally terrifying and she didn't know who to put her money on.

The bartender screamed and ran out.

"Gina, get her, erase the memory," Vint ordered.

Gina immediately followed the girl out and Hailey knew she needed to ask about that trick later. Right now she couldn't think about anything beyond the two demons squaring off at the bar.

Grail and Belinzar backed away from each other then threw what appeared to be balls of light in the other's direction; Grail's red and Belinzar's white. The lights met in the middle and clashed, disappearing in a sparkling show of power that filled the room with a tingling heat. It was intense and Hailey felt droplets of sweat form on her face.

"What the hell are we supposed to do?" She looked over and realized Mr. Pentack was also gone now, he must have followed Gina outside. Batal noticed as well and took off out the door quick as a flash. Hailey looked at Vint and bit her lip, wanting to run but also not wanting to leave if they could help.

Vint looked undecided. "Grail should be fine; they are a pretty even match."

"I don't think so," she hissed, holding her hand to her chest as it burned. "I think he is using me to help him."

Vint's eyes narrowed at his father. "Damnit," he snapped then started throwing his own hands up. Red bolts of power erupted from his palms and rushed toward Belinzar. Belinzar was caught off guard by the second attack and was knocked back. It was the opening Grail needed, throwing more at the demon. Together father and son managed to get enough hits on the other demon that he disappeared. Just poofed out of existence.

Vint rushed over to Hailey and grabbed the hand she was still cradling to her chest. He inspected the smooth skin then turned and punched Grail in the face.

The larger demon didn't move from the impact, but he didn't respond in kind either.

"Don't *ever* put her at risk like that again," Vint snarled.

"It was for her protection. I wasn't expecting to meet Belinzar while I enjoyed this nice bar," Grail defended, but there was a hint of regret in his eyes when he glanced her way.

Hailey touched Vint's shoulder and he relaxed, turning back to her.

"Are you alright?" Hailey asked Vint.

"Of course, are you alright?" Vint asked.

"I'm fine. Is Belinzar dead?"

"No, just went back to the demon realm. Whatever deal he had with Mr. Pentack, it wasn't to the death," Vint said. "A demon will always protect himself first. He knew he was losing so he left."

"You were quick on your feet, Vint," Grail admitted. "Though if Hailey had thrown some power at the thing it would have been faster. I might have been able to avoid this," he said pointing to a seeping wound in his side.

"Oh shit," she said, hurrying to him. "Vint, grab a rag from behind the bar."

"And some vodka," Grail added.

"It looks like a burn," she said as she inspected the wound.

"Feels like one too."

Hailey rolled her eyes at the big demon. "Why do you think I could have done anything to help?" she asked quietly while Vint rummaged behind the bar.

"You were practicing all day, didn't Vint show you some tricks to protect yourself?"

"I can levitate a rock," she said.

"A child's game," Grail snorted.

"She isn't powerful enough unless she embraces the magic fully. She can't do much else," Vint defended, handing her the rag.

Grail grabbed the bottle of vodka and dumped it on the wound then took the rag from Hailey and swiped. "I'll live," he declared.

Batal and Gina came in then. "We erased the girl's memory and saw Mr. Pentack take off like the rat he is," Gina sneered.

"I don't think we are done seeing him," Hailey sighed. "We need to be home, and no one goes on drinking adventures anymore," she snapped, pointing at Grail. "Not until this whole thing is done."

"What about your sister?" Vint said.

Hailey bit her lip. She felt like she was alone in this, like she was the one in charge and responsible, but it wasn't true, Kathy was just as vulnerable even if she wanted to deny the whole thing. "I think we need to at least warn her. Maybe we can convince her to come back to the house," Hailey sighed heavily. "And figure this shit out once and for all before any innocents get hurt."

"Are you saying I'm not innocent?" Grail scoffed.

"I imagine not since the invention of fire," she responded dryly and the demon laughed heartily. "Summer's shop isn't far, let's go there first. Grail, put on a shirt and cover the blood," Hailey ordered.

"Yes, Ma'am," he said with a condescending salute. He snapped his fingers and he was once again looking like a human —fully clothed too.

EIGHTEEN

When they got to Summer's family's shop they sat in the car a moment, observing the area for any coven members. None in sight.

Grail and Batal decided to stand watch outside while Vint and Gina accompanied Hailey inside.

The door chimed as they entered, alerting the salespeople that they had a customer. No one was in the main room of the little shop.

"Be right there!" Summer called from the back.

"It's just us," Hailey called back, not wanting her to rush whatever she might be doing.

"Wow, Vint check this shit out," Gina said as she leaned over a glass case. "These are legit."

"That's all Kathy's stuff," Hailey said.

"These are some powerful pieces, I bet the coven is all over this and Summer isn't charging enough," Gina said.

"Not charging enough for what?" Summer asked, coming out of the back.

"These pieces. Kathy has imbued them with magic, that one there is a spell enhancer," Gina said, pointing at a circular silver medallion with a gold star set into it. "And that one there protects the wearer from spells cast to harm them financially," she said, pointing to one that was a teardrop shape with amethyst shards embedded.

"Are you certain she wasn't trained by someone?" Vint asked.

"Naturally talented," Hailey assured them.

"See something you like?" Kathy asked, walking in.

"Who taught you to do this?" Vint asked.

"No one taught me. Well, I guess Grandma showed me a few basics of jewelry making when I was young and had an interest. But the designs are all my own. I draw them up and make them."

"You draw them first? Can I see?" Gina asked casually but something in her tone told Hailey it was anything but a casual inquiry.

"Yeah, I'll grab my sketchbook."

Kathy hurried into the back and returned with an old leatherbound sketchbook. Hailey recognized the worn beige cover with the gold design on the front of a fountain and a tree.

"That's a spell book," Vint said immediately.

"What? No, it's just a sketchbook," Kathy said with a snort.

"No, I can feel it from here. That is a book designed to assist a witch in the creation of spells. He's right," Gina said. "Your grandmother gave me a similar one. It was black with a silver crow on the front holding a chalice."

"She did give me this one for my eighteenth birthday, but why would she give me something magical?" Kathy spoke with a confused frown.

"She obviously saw your potential," Vint said. "Even bound as you were, you were still doing magic. She'd see that and it doesn't surprise me at all that she'd do something sneaky to help you enhance what you had."

Hailey tried not to let that little thought make her feel like shit. Her grandmother obviously hadn't seen anything in her, had never given her any magic-making notebooks.

Grail opened the door and glared inside, Batal pushing into the room, too. "Why are you upset, what's going on?"

All eyes turned to Hailey. She glared down at her clenched fist.

"Can you turn this fucking thing off?" Hailey bit out between clenched teeth.

Grail shrugged and snapped his fingers. "No one is in danger?"

"No," Vint said, eyeing Hailey with narrowed eyes.

"Weird," Kathy said as Grail went back outside. "So what did you guys come here for? Looking for some jewelry?"

"Not exactly," Hailey said and explained what had occurred at the bar.

"Why the hell would you let him have some kind of creepy connection with you?" Kathy chastised and shook her head.

That action made Hailey feel small and stupid, she cringed back from her sister and looked down at her clutched fingers.

"It's not her fault, Kathy. Grail is a skilled demon, all he does is trick and take," Vint growled in her defense.

Hailey looked at him, drawing strength from his words. It was true—she'd probably been dumb to let him put a mark on her without clearly knowing what it did, but it wasn't as if she had been through this before, neither of them had, and anger started to replace her shame. What right did Kathy have to judge her so harshly? "This isn't exactly something I've done before, Kathy. I'm just trying to figure out what the *fuck* to do without Grandma." Tears spilled from Hailey's eyes, and she was horrified but powerless to stop them.

"Oh, sis," Kathy said quietly and embraced her. "I know, I'm sorry it's all just a lot, you know."

Hailey let out a loud wet sob. "I know, I'm just so scared of making the wrong choice."

"Can you make me this?" Gina said, interrupting the sisterly moment without a thought or care, looking at the two of them with a bright smile.

Vint glared at her and Summer harumphed.

"What?" Gina said, genuinely confused by everyone's reaction.

"Geez, read the room, Gina," Vint grumbled.

Kathy pulled away and wiped the tears from Hailey's eyes with a reassuring smile. Then she turned to the inconsiderate half-demon. "Which design?" Kathy asked, sniffling back her emotions.

Gina held the open book up for them to see. "In silver with a pearl here."

The image was of an oval with a diamond in the center and a space for some kind of stone at the top of the diamond.

Summer giggled. "I remember when you drew that one. It was after our trip to Cancun and that nude beach resort."

"That's a vagina," Vint said dryly.

"Duh," Gina said. "It's a sexuality medallion. I think since my dad is a sex demon maybe if I work more on that side of things, I'll find more of my power."

"I think you came close last night," Batal said with a grin.

"I came twice last night," Gina agreed with a laugh.

"TMI and damn am I glad Hailey didn't call in *her* dad," Summer whispered.

"Sounds like it would be more like calling in *daddy*," Kathy said and erupted into a fit of laughter.

Hailey gaped at her sister momentarily then burst out in laughter as well, it was better than crying.

"Don't joke. He's seriously deadly," Gina grumbled.

"Speaking of deadly, who's watching the house if everyone is here?" Summer asked.

"Fuck," Hailey said.

"So you all just left the magic unattended, unguarded, unprotected?" Kathy said, her voice getting screechy by the end.

Hailey looked at Vint and bit her lip. Why had none of them thought of that as an issue. "It's probably fine ..." Hailey said.

Vint looked nervous and her confidence faltered.

Vint could have kicked himself, how did he not think of this, why had he allowed everyone to just leave the house unattended?

When they arrived back to Merry's house there were coven members lined up along the fence line staring in at the house. The house was pulsing with dark magic, demon magic. It tasted familiar to Vint. "Pentack and Belinzar," he snarled.

"You decided this was a better option," Mrs. Hilltop snapped at Hailey as they approached the gate.

"No I—I was trying to help someone, and this was unexpected."

"Demons are trouble, so you should have expected this, we did," Mrs. Hilltop snapped then turned and walked away, all of the coven members followed, each shooting her an accusing glare as they went. None offering to help.

"Fuck them," Grail snarled.

Vint felt their accusation and it filled him with shame.

Hailey, that's what he'd been thinking. She'd been in danger because of Grail's bond and his only thought had been to stop it, to make sure she was okay. He hadn't thought of anything else, hadn't cared about anything else. Not even the magic was more important than Hailey he realized, and the knowledge surprised him.

Grail slapped him on the back and leaned close to whisper. "You know this isn't going to end well, right?"

"Yeah," he said with clenched teeth. But he also knew he couldn't just walk away from the magic he'd wanted for so long. He looked over at Hailey and realized it was even more than that. He couldn't walk away and disappoint her; he wanted her to feel good about whatever direction the magic took, and this was definitely not going to make her feel good.

"What the hell do we do?" Hailey asked.

"Give up or go in," Grail said with a shrug.

"I do not give up," Hailey said firmly.

"So we walk up and see what he wants, maybe throw a few punches or magical balls of energy," Batal said, and Gina cracked her knuckles, ready for a fight.

"This is *my* fucking house," Hailey snarled and opened the gate.

Vint wanted to grab her and pull her back, keep her safe, but he just followed, knowing that she'd resent him trying to tell her what to do. She'd been protected all her life; kept vulnerable, out of love. What she needed was encouragement and strength to discover what she could be.

On the porch, Pentack stood with his demon beside him, both smiling, with an aura of dark magic vibrating around them. Vint could see it, but he wasn't sure Hailey did, and it was probably why she wasn't more scared. He dared a glance at Grail who was looking grim, he obviously didn't trust their odds here and Vint wondered how long it would be before the selfish demon cut ties with Hailey and went back to the demon realm to save himself.

"What the hell are you doing here, Pentack?" Hailey demanded.

"I decided that I would just take what I want, because why not, you can't stop me."

"Maybe I couldn't have when I was a student in your third-grade classroom but I'm a grown woman now and I am not going to let you talk down to me. And I am not alone," she snapped back.

To Vint's surprise she managed to lift a chair from the porch and it flew toward Pentack. He blocked it easily, but it was a good distraction. Grail jumped forward and engaged the other demon in a battle while Pentack charged toward Hailey. He lifted a hand and threw a glob of black magic at her. Vint pushed her aside and she fell to the ground while the spell continued on past them without harming anyone. The ground where it landed steamed and he had a feeling nothing would ever grow there again.

Hailey pointed a finger at the house and yelled, "Go inside."

Vint looked up at the house where she pointed, confused for a moment then realized Hailey was talking to the magic. It wasn't a bad idea, but he wasn't sure it would work. The air around the house seemed to shiver as if considering her order.

"Bitch," Pentack said and threw another magic ball at her, this one hit her thigh and she screamed.

The sound of Hailey's pain ripped the last of Vint's control to shreds and he threw his body at the man without a plan. He had no hesitation in hitting an old man who could throw magic like that and he went right for the guy's neck, smacking into it with a spell sizzling over his palm.

Pentack made a strangled sound and the skin on his neck turned red and bubbled with a magic burn. Pentack's hands smacked at Vint's face and let loose his own skin burning spell that made Vint drop the witch.

As soon as Pentack was free of Vint's grip he pulled his fist back and landed a hard punch to Vint's jaw that sent him stumbling back. Without hesitation, Pentack launched another ball of magic at Hailey. This time Pentack's magic hit her in the side, and she fell to the ground with a weak cry that sent a wave of panic through Vint. He hurried to her side and dropped down to his knees. He growled at her closed eyes and his gaze swept to her chest, the rise and fall reassuring, but she was obviously unconscious from the hit.

"Get her out of here," Grail snarled and threw everything he had at Belinzar. Gina and Batal jumped forward to block Pentack's further attacks on Hailey.

Vint didn't have time to think about what was best or what he was leaving behind. He picked Hailey up then ran to the only place he knew she'd be safe from Pentack and all the other witches.

"Don't you fucking die," he snapped, cradling her soft limp body against his chest as he ran

Vint stepped through the portal to his home. She needed what he could do for her, what he'd learned at the side of her grandmother, and he'd cultivated in his years alone. She was passed out, bleeding, and burned, the smell of her charred flesh and blood infiltrated his nostrils and made him cringe. But he would do anything to save her, this was Hailey Silver, the granddaughter of the woman he respected the most in the world and that was enough to want to save her. The desire to bring her here, to hold her away from anyone else who might help was something else, something demon.

He took her straight to his bed and laid her on the black comforter. He stripped off her shirt and pants, exposing the wounds that he would be healing.

"Fuck, Hailey, I am so sorry. If I had just let you have the magic … If I had encouraged your instincts, this never would have happened."

He wanted to punish himself but he didn't have time, she

needed healing, now. He went to the kitchen and rummaged for the ingredients he would use moving from memory, no written recipes or spells. He had been through this a million times in his mind. He poured, mixed and ground ingredients until he had a bowl of poultice that would treat the burn and stop the bleeding. Then he made a tea that would help with the pain and keep her asleep. It's what she needed to truly heal.

He felt Merry's presence as he worked, remembered her words and how she used to make the same things by his side. "I'm sorry I let your granddaughter get hurt," he whispered as he finished. "But I swear I will spend the rest of my life making up for it."

Rushing back to the bedroom he was shaking. The sight of her suffering and wounded made him want to scream, lash out and kill. His instincts of protection toward her were so above anything he'd ever thought possible, and he was barely thinking as he slathered the wounds with the poultice, covered them with clean cloths, and then pulled a sheet over her naked body. He spooned as much tea as she would allow into her mouth next, knowing she needed to heal from both the inside and the outside.

She never opened her eyes as he worked, never even moved, aside from the slight swallowing, and when he was done, when he knew he could do no more than wait, he dropped to his knees beside the bed and begged whatever gods might listen to a half-demon that she survive, that she live through this because she deserved everything and if she woke up he would give it to her without a fight, he'd go away and let her have the magic. Desperation clawed at him. He would do anything to save her.

CHAPTER

NINETEEN

Hailey woke slowly, images she couldn't quite place flitted through her head. There was a fight, magic was used, and she'd been hit.

She couldn't remember then.

She groaned and tried to roll over but her body hurt and the room smelled way too much like Vint. Had she been dreaming about him and somehow manifested his scent here? Where was here?

She cracked one eye open and immediately knew where she was. This was Vint's bedroom.

She sat up and the sheet pooled to her waist revealing she was naked in Vint's bed. She hurt, the pain keeping the embarrassment away at least for the moment. She investigated her body. Parts of her ribs and thigh were covered in cloths. She was afraid to look under them, remembering the pain of the hits she'd taken. Had Vint brought her here to help her? Why and how long ago? Shouldn't she have gone to a hospital? Where was everyone, who else was hurt and what had become of her grandmother's house? What about the magic?

She'd felt the magic so strongly while they fought, it had

seemed like it was trying to reach for her but it couldn't, like Pentack and his creepy demon were blocking it somehow. But that meant that they hadn't claimed it yet either, maybe it wasn't too late.

She swung her legs over the side of the bed and grimaced. She wasn't healed but she was determined to get answers. She lifted the edge of the cloth on her thigh to inspect the wound, it was buried beneath a thick poultice of herbs that smelled delicious and reminded her of her grandmother's soothing remedies. She wasn't sure she'd be able to get far without disturbing it, so she hesitated to leave the bed and debated calling out for help. But she was afraid Vint would be the one to answer and she was naked with no clothes in sight.

She pulled the blanket up to her chin and listened, hoping to hear her sister and Summer and everyone else, but there was only silence. Did that mean Vint had done this alone? Were the others just as harmed as her, perhaps not awakened yet ... or worse ...

Just as her thoughts started to spiral to the darkest things possible, the door opened and Vint stood there looking haggard. His shirt was a mess, bloody and wrinkled, his jeans the same. His hair was tousled, and his face looked wrecked. He'd taken a punch to the jaw and it was black and blue and there were red handprints on each of his cheeks. He looked at her with surprise in his strained eyes. He looked exhausted.

"You're awake!"

"Who else is hurt?" she demanded, she needed to know before anything else.

"No one."

Relief flooded her and she sunk back into the bed a bit. "The house?"

Vint just shook his head.

"We need to go; we need to get the house and the magic."

Determined to do just that she started to stand, gripping the blanket like her life depended on it.

"No!" Vint said, rushing forward and gently pushing her shoulders until she sat back down. "You need to heal; you are not ready to get up yet."

"Vint, I appreciate the care you've given me, but I am not going to let the others fight alone."

"They aren't," he assured her and picked up a cup of tea from the bedside. "Drink this, it will help with the pain."

She wasn't as comforted by that as she'd have liked to be. Had everyone given up? Were they just screwed? Pentack wins? She took the cup from Vint, recognizing the smell of it as the tea her grandmother always gave her for headaches. She sipped it, needing the relief; her side and thigh ached, her head pounded, and she couldn't even begin to make decisions until she eased the pain a bit.

"How long have I been here?"

"I brought you here about three hours ago."

"Just you?" she asked, her cheeks heating.

"Yeah. I know how to heal, your grandmother taught me."

Hailey looked down at the blanket covering her naked body. So he'd definitely seen ... everything. She looked back at him unsure how to ask if he'd been a gentleman and avoided leering at her breasts while cleaning her wounds.

Vint looked guilty. "Hailey we ... we had to back off ... you were hurt and ... well no one could fight what he was doing. He had so much power."

That's not what she'd been so worried about in the moment but now that he was on the subject she was back to worrying about it. "My power! He is stealing my power, Kathy's power."

"I know," Vint gritted.

"So you all just gave up," Hailey gasped.

"We had no choice, Hailey. You would have bled out up

there. You couldn't have taken another hit and he knew it. He was going after you hard because he could tell you are the one holding onto the magic the hardest."

"I won't let him have my grandmother's magic," she snarled. "I'd rather you have it than that jackass."

Vint smiled. "Thanks, I think."

"Where is everyone else?"

"They are keeping an eye on the house, but they are not engaging."

"We have to stop him."

"It's most important that you heal."

"Vint we can't—"

"We can't do anything!" Vint yelled and Hailey had never seen the half-demon look so intimidating. "We can't do anything, or you and Kathy will be killed. You don't know anything about the magic; you barely have any to use, and I am nothing but a half-demon. I am no match for a witch with that kind of battery power behind him and his demon sidekick."

Hailey glared at Vint. "Wow, really feeling sorry for yourself huh?"

Vint looked at her with shock.

"You aren't powerful enough?" she scoffed. "You are a fucking demon *and* a witch! We have another demon witch on our team and a full demon! Batal too, though I'm not really sure how helpful he might be. I am not willing to walk away, and I doubt Kathy is either. So decide if you're helping or not, but you won't stop me from fighting for what's mine." Maybe something had broken in her brain when she'd been hit, she wasn't sure, but the thought of dying to keep the power was better than the thought of living, knowing she'd just walked away a coward.

"What do you expect me to do?" Vint gritted.

"I expect you to find me something to wear and take me

back out of here. I can't imagine it will take long for the magic to be stolen. Shit, I probably need to let Kathy know I'm alive. She's probably heard about the fight by now, knows we fucking failed Grandma and everyone else."

Vint's look told her she was right.

"At the moment Pentack can only use the magic he can't really possess it, but he was working on it."

"Then we have no time to lose, get me a shirt," Hailey demanded.

An hour later Hailey was dressed in a pair of Vint's sweats and T-shirt, her wounds were bandaged fresh and they were sitting in Kathy and Summer's apartment. Grail was there too, but Gina and Batal were outside of her grandmother's house keeping watch.

"I think it's enough, this is enough," Summer said. "You are hurt, you were almost killed, this is crazy, right?"

Hailey met Kathy's gaze across the room. Her sister had been very quiet since they arrived. After the initial phone call freakout, she'd been deep in thought, and Hailey wasn't sure what to expect her to say.

"Grandma would never want someone like Mr. Pentack to have her magic. Magic that is our birthright, our heritage." Kathy met Hailey's gaze across the room then turned to Summer. "I'm sorry, hun, but I can't just let that happen, you know I can't."

Summer sighed heavily and sank into the couch next to Kathy. "I knew you were going to say that. Okay, what do we do?" Summer directed the question at Grail.

"Is that the decision? You two are keeping the magic?" Grail asked.

"No!" Hailey said quickly. "No, no decision made. You are not released from your agreement to help me."

Grail smiled at her. "Okay then, in the interest of helping you make a decision, we need to go to the house, and we need to surround it, make a witch circle, draw the power away from the house. Then we can take Pentack and his demon on with a more even playing field."

"We'd need a whole coven for that," Vint scoffed.

"Is that not what you are?" Grail said casually, looking down at his fingernails in disinterest. "A coven of four is a coven all the same and can share magic even."

Hailey opened her mouth and clamped it shut, was he implying what she thought he was implying? She met Vint's gaze across the room and saw the same thoughts reflected in his eyes.

"Will it work?" Kathy demanded.

"It might," Vint whispered. "But it is still dangerous. It would be great if we had something extra on our side."

"Like some kind of protective medallions?" Summer said, practically jumping in her seat. "Kathy, you probably have something at the shop!"

"I'm not ... I don't ... ugh, yeah, I probably do," Kathy said shaking her head.

"It's okay, Kathy. I don't think you embracing this is a bad thing," Summer assured her.

Kathy met Summer's gaze and shook her head. "You'll still love me if I'm a witch?"

"I'll love you even if you're a demon. Kathy, it won't change who you are on the inside."

Kathy kissed Summer. "Okay, let's do this," Kathy said.

. . .

A quick stop at the shop and they were prepared to fight. With Vint and Grail's help Kathy had gathered four medallions she'd made that would protect and amplify their abilities. They were all a little different but apparently, they worked about the same as each other. Gina got one shaped like a triangle with a branch through it that would help her to stay grounded and pull fertility magic from the earth. Vint got one that was shaped like a half-moon and star, meant to help him focus the darker elements of his magic. Hailey got one shaped like a shooting star meant to help her gather the magic that trailed around her. And Kathy got one shaped like a circle with a flower meant to assist her in accepting her inner gifts. They all had a protective element as well and as they stood together holding the medallions around their necks it really did feel like they had an undeniable connection.

"A true coven is nothing more than a group of witches who agree to work together for the good of the group," Grail explained. "It will mean you can share power and work together. If you circle the house and work as a team, you should be able to pull the magic out and hold it temporarily, keep it out of Pentack's reach long enough for me and Batal to go in. We take out Pentack and his demon pal and then you let the magic back down."

"Sounds too easy, but also too dangerous for you two," Hailey said, pointing to Batal and Grail.

"Batal will go as a cat, sneak up and attack from behind. All I need to do is get a couple good hits in on his demon and he'll split, just like he did at the bar. Demons are self-serving above all else, remember. He won't die for Pentack no matter what the witch promised him."

Hailey bit her lip, it didn't seem right, sending Batal and Grail in to do the hard work. But she also knew her limits, she couldn't fight physically, and she wasn't strong or sure enough in her magic to really do any damage against what Pentack and Belinzar threw.

They parked a few houses down from Merry's home, the sun had set a while ago and with the cover of the cloudy night they slunk toward the house. Hailey could feel the pulsing of magic around it. Not the comforting feeling she'd always gotten from her grandmother's home; this was tainted, and she worried they were already too late.

But then she sensed something else, a presence, it felt as familiar and welcoming as her grandmother's arms, but she knew it wasn't a ghost of the woman she missed with her entire being. It was the magic that had been so much a part of her grandmother and yet Hailey hadn't known it for what it was.

The magic was reaching out to her, calling to her and she was reassured.

"He hasn't taken it yet," she whispered to the others.

"No, I can feel it reaching out," Kathy said with awe. "It's so weird and yet so familiar. I can't even explain it."

Hailey nodded in agreement; they had a lot to learn.

"Okay, let's do this, no one gets hurt, okay, run before you put yourself into any real danger," Hailey ordered.

Grail snorted. "I'm a demon, I live for this shit."

"I thought you lived to devour your offspring," Hailey teased, and Grail gave her a lopsided grin and a wink before transforming into his large demon form.

Kathy and Summer gasped and stepped back; they hadn't witnessed this amazing thing yet.

"He won't hurt us," Hailey assured them.

"Speak for yourselves," Vint said with a growl.

With the plan set and no time to waste, Hailey hugged Kathy then they all moved. Summer was to stay at the vehicles where she'd be safe and able to keep any neighbors or curious walkers away from danger. Kathy gave her a passionate kiss before running to her point at the southwestern corner of the house. Hailey was taking the northeastern, Vint the southeastern and Gina the northwestern.

Batal and Grail ran for the front door and as soon as they were inside the circle that was going to be set, the four witches started to connect.

Hailey reached out, one hand toward Vint and the other toward Gina. She reached down inside herself and touched the part of herself that was buzzing with energy, eager to connect with more magic. She let it flow up out of her belly and into her arms, to her palms and further, pushing it toward the two half-demons.

She felt Vint's magic first, it was like a hot splash full of anger and resentment but also something else, something deeper, something sad. Gina's was a tingle of heat, full of lust, desire, and sadness, raw and open. Where Vint buried everything, it seemed Gina let it all out and embraced it.

The combination was almost overwhelming, Hailey swayed on her feet.

"Keep it going!" Vint yelled in her direction, obviously sensing her struggle and she wondered how Kathy was doing on the other side.

Hailey had a clear view of the front of the house, and she focused there as they let the power between them build and the bond strengthen.

Batal and Grail didn't stop, Grail slammed into the front door, and it splintered. Hailey gasped at the show of strength. Then there was a black blast of power and Grail and Batal were thrown out of the house, stumbling and rolling across the porch and onto the lawn.

"Shit, we can't wait any longer," Vint yelled out.

"He's using the magic, isn't he?" Hailey yelled across to Vint who nodded gravely.

It was on Hailey and Kathy mostly now. They were going to pull the magic while Vint and Gina supported them with their own magic then release it back to the house. Pentack was going to be holding it tight though and it would take more than a simple decision to pull the magic around. There was a possibility that they'd have to take it in, but that was a last resort.

Fear and excitement coiled in Hailey's belly, this was it, this was a moment that could change everything, and she didn't know what life would look like after, but she wanted to know. She suddenly wanted the magic fully without question.

She closed her eyes as Batal and Grail stood and headed back toward the house ready to engage and distract. She couldn't watch, was too afraid she'd see them harmed and she'd falter in her concentration.

Vint growled and hissed as he felt the magic start to enter the women on either side of him. The magic that he had coveted for so long, the magic he'd always thought would be his. But he'd been kidding himself, he realized that now. No one in their right mind would turn down the kind of life altering power that was here, even Kathy, afraid as she was to change anything in her seemingly perfect life she'd created, was open and embracing the tendrils of power that were entering her. Vint could feel Kathy's joy and hesitant excitement.

A fierce growl ripped across the yard and Vint saw Grail engage with Belinzar in hand-to-hand combat. The only possible reason for that was that Belinzar didn't really want to win, didn't care to destroy Grail. He was just barely doing his agreed upon task.

"Typical demon," Vint said with a half smile because this time, it worked in their favor.

Grail took a hit to the chin and Vint saw blood spray, but Grail was barely shaken, standing up straight and hitting back. Batal was small and fast, ducking and dodging everything Pentack threw his way. Every magical ball, every fist and foot. Vint could see the older witch's body start to sag, his energy sapping. It was too much; he couldn't engage in a physical fight while holding onto the magic that was trying to leave.

"We can do this, don't stop!" Vint yelled reassurance to the women who were both looking strained as they worked to pull in magic they didn't understand. Vint pushed his own power to them, aiding in their energy and boosting their pull. It was his and Gina's job to work as batteries for the two witches, pushing out, not taking in anything. He could feel his sister doing the same thing from her corner.

Vint focused back to the fight just in time to see Grail take a hit from the demon and Pentack at the same time.

Where the hell was Batal?

But then he saw the cat man, rushing across the yard.

"What the fuck?" Vint yelled but Batal didn't stop. He was barreling toward where Gina was and that's when Vint felt it, the break in their circle.

Something had happened to Gina; it was the only thing that would have Batal running away from the fight.

"Shit!" Vint screamed and he felt the panic of the sisters as the circle broke and the magic started to fade. "Pull!" Vint screamed. He knew what he had to do as Grail struggled to stand and was hit double again.

Hailey was going to hate him.

TWENTY

Hailey panicked; she didn't know what to do. She felt a sharp cut off from Gina and when her eyes flew open. She saw the demon witch lying unconscious, and behind her stood James Connery, coven member and gardener, with a hammer in his hand and a smug smile on his face.

She almost ran for Gina but then she saw the flash of Batal heading in her direction and heard Vint yelling at her to pull. She wanted to cry but she didn't move, didn't help Gina, she left it to Batal and did as Vint instructed. The magic she'd been feeling was cut in half now and she felt so weak, but she did as Vint told her. She pulled with everything she had, pulled and screamed with anger at her parents for denying her the easy way, for her grandmother making the will unclear, and for the coven making everyone's life harder than it had to be. She raged at the unfairness of Vint and Gina's struggles and the looming threat to Summer and Kathy's future.

With one final *fuck you* to all of it, she gave over her last bit of energy. She felt Vint's strength bolster her. Together, they pulled.

The magic dumped into her with a sudden flash that first

chilled then heated her body. All sound and sight blacked out for a moment, her nerves all alight with new knowledge and new energy. Then it was all gone. She felt nothing and she opened her eyes to see Grail bloody but standing. He gave her a nod and disappeared.

It was done, the magic had settled.

She collapsed.

Hailey groaned as she rolled, inhaling the familiar scent of lavender and dust. She was in her room at her grandmother's house. She'd had the weirdest dream she'd ....

She sat up with a gasp and a groan as every muscle in her body protested the movement. Valerie in her ghostly form stood at the end of the bed watching her.

"Oh good. You're awake. I'll alert them."

"Them?" Hailey croaked but the maid was already gone, and Hailey fell back to the bed.

She didn't have long to wonder, her door opened and in walked Gina and Batal, bright smiles and worried eyes.

"Are you okay?" Batal asked.

"I think so, but Gina, you were knocked out," Hailey said, sitting up again, slower this time. "Are *you* okay?"

"Yeah, asshole snuck up on me. He knocked Summer out too."

"Shit, is she okay?" The one fully human of them all. They never should have let her anywhere near the fight.

"Fine, she's got a headache, but she'll be alright. Vint made her some healing tea and she's with Kathy. He's got a knack for the healing thing."

"How's Kathy?"

"Same as you. She passed out from the power influx but is

awake now," Vint said from the doorway where he lurked, looking guarded and unsure.

"We did it?" she asked, although she was pretty sure they had, otherwise they wouldn't be in the house.

"Yeah, we'll leave you two alone," Gina said and pulled Batal out of the room.

Hailey frowned and scooted back on the bed, leaning against the pillows. "What? Did it not work? I saw Grail disappear. He went home because the decision was made, right? He wasn't just running away?"

"We lost Gina's help when she was hit, the power she and I were supplying to your and Kathy's effort was halved and with Batal out of the fight Grail wasn't going to be able to keep both Belinzar and Pentack distracted for long," Vint started, pacing to the window and back to the bed.

"Right, I was there, remember," she said with a forced laugh, did he think she'd addled her brain somehow?

"I panicked," Vint continued with a frown. "I felt you and Kathy both turn indecisive. I felt you both start to fade and ..."

"And?" Hailey demanded. Concern welled up when Vint didn't continue.

Vint closed his eyes and took a steadying breath. "I started to pull."

Hailey narrowed her eyes at him, knowing what he was saying, that wasn't the deal, he wasn't supposed to pull any of the magic. He and Gina were supposed to act as batteries for her and Kathy, that was it. Then he and Gina were supposed to help push the magic back to the house so they could all make one final decision without threat of death.

"But I felt it, the magic entered me. It was like a splash, a consuming dump. I felt it," she whispered the last, confused. Vint hadn't taken it, she knew she'd taken it. She did a quick body check and she could swear she felt it in her now even.

Vint looked at her and nodded. "I didn't know it was possible, but the magic, it entered all three of us. It shouldn't have been able to, we aren't family, you can share magic with family, blood family or your coven. We aren't a real coven; we shouldn't have been able to share it." His voice was panicked as he explained.

"Fuck," Hailey said more out of awe than anger. "Well, I guess we should have figured that could happen," she laughed. "I think Grail knew."

Vint didn't hide the surprise on his face. "You're not angry?"

She shook her head. "Why would I be? This is like the perfect solution, we should have thought of this first, why not just share it? But what about Gina?"

"She was disconnected from our circle when we pulled the magic, so she didn't get any. But she's still a part of us. I can feel her there like I never did before despite us being half related."

Hailey thought about it all and grinned. "We are a real coven. That's so cool. It makes us stronger, doesn't it? And I don't know," she shrugged. "It feels right, like maybe this is what Grandma wanted all along."

Vint smiled at her, a genuine full smile that lit up his face in a way that made Hailey's heart flutter and her stomach tingle.

"I think you're right."

"Does Kathy know?"

"Yeah, she took it well, but I think she was just glad she didn't get all that magic dumped into her. She's a little scared of it still I think."

"That's because she's always been too practical, so focused on her idea of what life and the future should be. This is unexpected and she doesn't always handle unexpected well."

"And you're supposedly the nervous one?" Vint scoffed.

Hailey shrugged and smiled at him. Everything felt right.

"What are you going to do about all this angst you have going on?" Gina asked as Vint sat with her in the sunroom. Hailey was gardening in front of the house and no one else was around.

"What are you talking about?" Vint said, but he did know. It had been nearly a week since they'd settled into this new arrangement and his desire for Hailey had only grown.

"You *are* good enough for her," Gina said quietly. "You are the most caring big brother I could have asked for. You supported Merry whenever she needed. You are a good man, Vint."

"I'm a half-demon."

"Me too, does that mean I don't deserve love?"

"Of course not!" Vint turned to his sister and gave her a fierce look, if anyone deserved love it was her. She was powerful, thoughtful and fun. Anyone would be lucky to keep her.

She smiled, "I know, and so do you, Vint. Hailey would be lucky to have you."

Vint turned to look out at the yard. "It's not the same."

"Why? Because you have a dick? Trust me, they aren't that impressive. I've seen plenty."

"Gross," Vint said rolling his eyes. He was used to his sister's casual treatment of sex but that didn't mean he liked to hear about it.

Gina laughed. "All I'm saying is that if you think being a half-demon isn't a terrible thing then what's stopping you from going after what you want? Everyone has noticed the way you watch her, well everyone except her. I think she might be a bit clueless."

Vint had tried hard to keep his feelings hidden, he hated that apparently, he was so bad at it.

"She deserves to have everything."

"Yeah, she does," Gina agreed. "Including the option to date you, if that's what she wants, and you shouldn't take that choice away from her."

Gina walked away and Vint was left feeling like a huge weight had just dropped on his shoulders. Everyone knew, everyone was waiting to see what he would do. If he did nothing, he should just leave so he wouldn't have to eventually watch her with someone else. That thought made him think of murder with a smile. She would hate him if he started killing people she dated. She'd be better off if he just left, wouldn't she? But something Gina had said really struck him; choice. It was something Hailey valued, having choices, not being told what was good for her.

There was really only one solution.

"Merry, forgive me, but I think I might want to ask your granddaughter out on a date." He cringed even as he said it out loud. What would Merry have said?

He hoped she'd approve.

"Sir, if I may interrupt," Drandy said appearing in the room with him. He hated that the servants lurked so often he forgot to watch out for them.

"I suppose you already have," Vint said.

"Merry spoke of you highly and she always wanted you and your sister to have everything possible for your future. I don't think that stopped at finding a true love with her granddaughter."

Vint smiled at the old ghost. "Thank you, Drandy."

"But if you hurt her, I will kill you myself," he said and disappeared.

Vint laughed because he would expect nothing less from anyone who knew Hailey, she was a woman worth killing for.

Hailey sat on the front porch sipping coffee. The front door was repaired and despite her desire to finally add in that window she'd always thought her grandmother needed, she'd repaired it back to its original solid state. Mrs. Hilltop stopped at the gate, her little dog barking at a squirrel.

"Morning, Mrs. Hilltop," Hailey said to the coven member.

"Morning, Hailey," she said with a sigh. "I wanted to let you know that James has been properly punished for his actions, stripped of his magic and kicked out of the coven for helping Mr. Pentack."

That surprised Hailey but she had been very insistent that if the coven didn't want enemies of their newly formed and unusual coven—arguably more powerful due to its demon members—they would be taking care of things and they would act respectfully to all members, demon and not. The terms were agreed to, but Hailey wasn't sure they'd actually follow through.

The threat of no more tea if they didn't was probably what sealed the deal.

Mrs. Hilltop moved on, and a black cat came to sit by Hailey.

"Good morning, Batal. Did you have mice for breakfast or are you hungry, I think Summer cooked bacon and egg casserole."

Batal morphed into his human form and scoffed. "I don't eat mice."

"But you chase them," she pointed out.

"Yes, but they are not good on my digestion. I chase and catch. I don't consume."

"Well then, go get some breakfast before it's gone."

Batal hurried inside. He was never far from the house and Hailey wondered if he was a permanent resident she never invited. Gina was living in the house with her now and although Kathy and Summer were still in their own home, they were often here as was Vint who was teaching Hailey and Kathy how to use and control the new magic.

"I brought you a piece," Vint said, sitting beside her.

"Oh thanks," Hailey took the offered plate but didn't eat. Her stomach was twisting, as it always seemed to do when Vint was close. Now that things had settled, she didn't have anything to distract her from the fact that she was very much attracted to him.

She just didn't know if he felt the same and what would happen if they ruined this whole coven thing that was so new.

With a groan of frustration she sipped her coffee.

"What has you so twisted this morning?" Vint asked.

"Nothing, just thinking about what needs to be replanted where the magic-eaters destroyed the garden."

"Oh," Vint said. And was that disappointment she heard in his tone? "I can help, whatever you need."

"Sure, thanks."

"We could go to the nursery today, pick out a few things," Vint added.

"Yeah, I'll get dressed in a minute."

Vint cleared his throat, wringing his hands in his lap and shifted nervously. Hailey looked at him then and saw he had his eyes closed and was pressing his lips together as if he were about to do something terrible. Hailey's heart started to pound and worry snaked through her.

"Maybe we can grab some lunch too?" Vint said, still not opening his eyes, his voice strained. "Um, I'd like to buy you lunch, I mean, take you for lunch. I want to—"

Hailey giggled and Vint's eyes flew open.

"Vint D'red are you asking me out on a date?" she mock gasped.

He stood and turned back to the house. "It's fine, never mind."

"Hey!" she said and grabbed his leg making him stumble and nearly fall. "I didn't say no."

He dropped to his knees beside her, such raw hope and fear on his face Hailey wanted to bundle him in her arms and reassure him that there was nothing wrong with him, that he was perfect in his half-demon, half-witch form. She ran a hand over one of his horns and leaned in, giving him a quick kiss.

"I thought you'd never ask," she whispered against his lips.

Vint let out a pained groan and pulled her onto his lap. He pressed his lips hard against hers and she opened for him. His hot tongue swept into her mouth, and it was her turn to groan. The kiss was consuming, it melted her and lit her on fire. She couldn't stop herself from running both hands up to grab his horns.

He pulled away and looked at her with heavy lidded eyes, dark with passion. "I've wanted to do that since I first saw you in the doorway," he admitted.

"And I've been so damn curious about these," she said giving the horns a little stroke.

Vint let out another groan and pushed her away. "If you do too much of that, we won't make it to the nursery or lunch," he said firmly.

"Oh," her cheeks heated and her heart beat wildly. "They are sensitive?"

"I imagine it's a lot like me touching you here," he said and ran a hand lightly over her breast, her nipple already beaded with desire, tingled at the touch and she sucked in a sharp breath.

"Oh, well, good to know." Her cheeks reddened thinking of how she'd brazenly stroked him, and they hadn't even been on a date.

Vint leaned forward and kissed her cheek then moved to whisper in her ear. "You are so fucking perfect, Hailey. I want to do this right, so go get dressed before this demon is tempted to drag you to his house and never let you out again."

Why did those words send her into a near panting amount of desire? On wobbly legs Hailey got up and headed into the house.

One year later Hailey stood in the kitchen a little after midnight, making tea. She was very careful; she knew what she was trying to do. She pulled out black tea leaves, cinnamon and orange peel, she hummed happily and boiled the water. When the tea had steeped, she closed her eyes, set her intention and sipped.

"What the hell am I here for now?"

"Grail!" Hailey squealed and jumped at the demon, surprising him with her enthusiastic embrace.

"Well, hello, but why did you bring me back?" Grail pushed her back and frowned, his eyes darting around the room. "Are you in danger?"

"I brought you back to tell you that your son is getting married, and I think you should be there."

"Married? Why the hell would he do that?"

Hailey put her hands on her hips and glared at the big demon. "Because he fucking loves me, that's why."

"*You*! You are marrying Vint? Aw, come on, I thought you were smarter than that, the kid's half-demon and all disappointment." His words were harsh, but his tone was teasing.

"The man is wonderful, and kind, and I trust him with every part of myself."

"I see," Grail said with an eye roll. "So when is this thing happening?"

"Today," she said nervously. "In a couple hours actually."

Grail's eyes lit up with mischief. "He doesn't know I'm here, does he?"

"I want you to walk me down the aisle, Grail." She wanted to show Vint that he had support, that there was hope to make more peace in their lives, more connections to family. They'd been working together to offer assistance to any orphaned half-demon or abandoned witch for the last year and this was the next step. Hailey wanted a full demon who supported their cause. Grail had every reason to be that. She'd glimpsed goodness in him, no matter how small and deeply buried. "Will you?"

He sighed heavily but nodded agreement and she threw herself in his arms again.

"Stop doing that, I'm a fierce demon," he said but there was almost no real anger behind it.

"You are, but you're also a father, my friend, and soon ..." she touched her belly that had yet to start to round with the child inside.

"No shit, well fuck ... I guess I better get you two married then, can't have anyone thinking you're a loose woman."

Hailey hit his chest and glared. "Rude. Now go get changed into the suit I have for you in the bathroom. Ceremony is at sunrise."

It was a beautiful ceremony, everything Hailey could have asked for aside from her parents and grandmother being there, but she felt their presence all around her and it was comforting. Grail looked dashing in his suit and when Vint saw who was walking her down the aisle he glared until Grail gave her hand to Vint and spoke. "Take care of her, son. She's worth more than you and me both."

"I know," Vint said gruffly and looked at her.

Hailey was about to burst into tears. She blamed the pregnancy hormones, but it was also the look of shock, pain and hope that she saw flash across Vint's features. This was her gift to him, hope for a family that included everyone.

And when Vint and Hailey kissed for the first time as husband and wife, the crowd cheering, Vint filled Hailey with the same heat and desire as that first kiss on the front porch. She was so in love with this half-demon she could barely stand to keep her hands off of him. Which is why this wedding had been planned on such short notice.

He said she was perfect, but she thought he was too.

MEET THE AUTHOR

Courtney Davis is an award-winning author of speculative fiction romance: paranormal, dystopian, urban fantasy, and space. She loves creating worlds and exploring human and inhuman interactions.

She grew up and currently resides in North Idaho with her husband and children—teaching, reading, writing and soaking up sunshine.

She hopes you find joy and an escape in her writing.

OTHER TITLES FROM

5 PRINCE PUBLISHING